MacK
McKinnon, Karen,
Narcissus ascending

1st ed.

NARCISSUS

ASCENDING

NARCISSUS ASCENDING

Karen McKinnon

PICADOR USA

NEW YORK

www.picadorusa.com

Design by Philip Mazzone

Title page art: Getty Images, Inc.

"Cartography After Six Months." Copyright © 2002 by Peter Nickowitz. Reprinted by permission.

Grateful acknowledgement is given for permission to quote from the following lyrics:
"Imagination." Words by Johnny Burke. Music by Jimmy Van Heusen. © copyright 1939 by Bourne Co., Dorsey Bros. Music, Marke Music Publishing Co., Limerick Music Corp., My Dad's Songs, and Reganesque Music Company. Copyright renewed. All rights reserved. International copyright secured. All rights on behalf of Marke Music Publishing administered by BMG Songs, Inc. (ASCAP). All rights on behalf of Limerick Music Corp., My Dad's Songs, and Reganesque Music Company in the U.S. administered by Spirit Two Music, Inc. (ASCAP).

ISBN 0-312-29058-6

First Edition: June 2002

10   9   8   7   6   5   4   3   2   1

For my parents, Inell and Jim,
with love

Imprisoned in his pseudo-awareness of himself, the new Narcissus would gladly take refuge in an idée fixe, a neurotic compulsion, a "magnificent obsession"—anything to get his mind off his own mind.

—CHRISTOPHER LASCH,
The Culture of Narcissism: American Life
in an Age of Diminishing Expectations

Why do we have a mind if not to get our way?

—FYODOR DOSTOYEVSKY

NARCISSUS
ASCENDING

ME

I'm over it. I don't have to obsess about it anymore. Everyone comes to me about it now because I'm strong. And I remember.

She smiled extravagantly at me from the wall. Hugh's wall at Berkeley was smothered in Callie. 28 poses. All happy. Lying. Straight black hair stuck behind big ears, big eyes gemblue and there for you. Unless a mirror was in range. She had unerring radar for anything reflective. Wicked Queen. And Snow White, so pale, with freckles lightly scattered across that nose which she'd touch her fingers to incessantly after masturbating. We always knew when she'd been masturbating. It was the only time she wanted to be alone.

When Hugh visits, Callie straddles us. Neither of us has seen her in a good long time, and reciting the reasons for this has become part of how Hugh and I reconnect after long absences. On the bus from Newark Airport we repeat the ritual. Have you seen her? he begins. Not intentionally. I ran into her in the Village a couple of months ago. I was having a bad last argument with Steve, the one I went out with for half a year too long. I was crying and I looked up from my shoes which I was staring at to keep from screaming at Steve. Callie was walking toward me, alone, her eyes were gleaming at my distress. I was mortified to be caught failing at a relationship with no help from her. She didn't take her eyes off me once to look at Steve, wrapping me in those long arms of hers, holding me tight against the padding of her breasts. You let her? Hugh demands. He is trying to decide if I have betrayed him. I am trying to decide if I have confessed something.

Hugh is tired. His greygreen eyes are redrimmed which is not becoming this early in the glaring New York morning. He takes the redeye so that when we reach my apartment he can slip into my bed. This time it could actually lead to something. I watch him sleep. From the boudoirchair in the corner of my room I take inventory of my favorite parts of Hugh. His eyes are shut but I know they're there under the long girlish lashes. His lips are slightly parted, the color of my chair. The pink velvet needs recovering. I like coffee and I'm careless.

Hugh is dreaming. I see his lids flutter and figure he's with Callie now. I'd like to see inside his dream, see if it's like mine. She stands in front of a mirror trying in vain to see her own profile. She catches your eye, says You can touch me if you want.

Hugh did touch her, the shimmering surface of her. They were supposed to be married but then she went to Paris and everything fell apart. Except my wanting Hugh. His visit's revived it. His mouth opens wider and he pulls my comforter over his face.

I dial Dahlia. I whisper He's here. Dahlia knows Hugh from high school. Is there anyone left in California? Hugh and Dahlia had exactly one date which she cried through. They saw Terms of Endearment, it wasn't her fault.

I met Dahlia in New York, but we grew up 20 miles apart on The Left Coast, the one we left. Dahlia grew up fabulously. Her mother died of melanoma and her father consoled her with clothes and trips abroad and racehorses. We never would have met there. New York's good like that.

Dahlia's coming over. She'll grab a cab. She'll bring a box of orange juice because she doesn't want cancer. She wants me to give up coffee but I think I'll take my chances.

I wash my hair. I didn't wash it yesterday but I did the day before. It always looks best Day 2. Just the right amount of wave and not yet matted. I can't brush it. I'm not allowed. Dahlia says I brush too hard. I break my hair. Just run your fingers through it while it's wet is her advice. I listen to Dahlia. My hair's grown 6 inches since I met her. It falls down my back. It catches your eye. Dahlia says it's beautiful. I turn my back on myself in my steamy mirror, watch my ropey blonde waves roll across my back, wish I could see myself as Hugh sees me. I grab a hank of hair with each hand, face the mirror, let my hair fall over my chest, my breasts peak through the strands, I pull my fingers down their wetness. Will it happen this time with Hugh? Should it? I have to try to separate my longings. No one's seen me naked in months. I really miss being looked at, appreciated. I really miss being touched. No one's touched me that way in way too long. I'm turning into Dahlia. My intercom bleets. Dahlia's here. I buzz her in.

We watch Hugh sleep. Dahlia sits on the boudoir-chair and I sit on the rug with her fingers in my hair. She has huge hands and likes to rub my head with them. She keeps her fingernails short, for me. Dahlia's a dancer and also has big feet which I watch clench the rug as she rubs.

She whispers He's starting to lose his hair and I look up through mine which is thick and tumbled over. She's right. Hugh's careful do is undone on my big fat pillow. Maybe you should do him next Dahlia. My head is tingling.

I lean on Dahlia, let my head fall on her lap, let my muscles go all useless. She gives my head a push and I let it fall forward again, watch my hair cascade, feel it tickle my face. Blow. She keeps rubbing, kneading, using her tension to release mine. She acupressures me, forces me to find my life's pressure points. No one loves like Dahlia. We met through Callie so I didn't notice. Not till Callie was out of the way.

Dahlia's seen Callie but I didn't tell Hugh. That's between him and Dahlia. Dahlia has her own before and after with Callie which I hear about since I live here, but Hugh's stuck in California which is capital N nowhere in the realm of Callie.

Dahlia saw her at Lot 61. It was an accident. Callie was with a guy Dahlia knows from the Joyce and that's how it happened. Dahlia got stood up and Callie bought her drinks all night, telling Dahlia her date was an idiot.

Callie was sweet. Dahlia wasn't expecting it so her guard was down and she confessed to thinking Hey, it's really good to see her.

She's out there and we just never know when it'll be our turn. And when it happens, I'm the one who has to remind everyone how much work she is, how much trouble.

Hugh stirs, exposes his chest. It's narrow and hairless and looks like it would be soft. I'm thinking we should wake him up and get on with it. But through a skein of hair I see Dahlia put a finger to her lips so I keep quiet.

Dahlia wants to invite Max over to watch Hugh sleep. Max is the actor Callie left Hugh for, the one Dahlia had an affair with while she was living with Callie. Max is a great guy but I've never gone for brooding and leather.

Max and Hugh haven't met but they probably dream about each other. Maybe Dahlia's right. Maybe it's time to get them together. It might help them come to terms with Callie.

By extension, then, I should also invite Liz and her husband Stuart who took Callie out on Valentine's Days because that's when she always broke up with her lovers. And my ex Fred who would never come after what she did to him, and Fred's roommate who met Callie when she was doing quantity over quality. Then there was the old guy who owned that little Italian joint on Callie's block, the one who told us over Chianti that I was smarter and prettier than Callie so she slept with him.

I'm not sure all these people will fit in my apartment. I think we should keep it just us for now. Maybe Max but we'll see how things go.

Dahlia lets go of my head and I pat her knee. Thanks, that was great. Shh. She's protective of Hugh. He does look fragile, and he's twitching. I nod and leave Dahlia on the chair. I'll make coffee. We could have a long wait for Hugh.

I should be used to it. When I got to Berkeley, Callie was gone but her effect wasn't. There were the pictures, sure, but that wasn't the worst of it. She'd made a lasting impression. People at the coop aka Institute for Cooperative Living were downright smitten. So many synonyms for vivacious. And funny and raucous. All the things I wasn't. That was a long time ago. I'm over it.

Grinding the beans is my favorite part of making coffee. It's quickly violent and it smells good. And at this point in the morning it's all for me. When Hugh wakes up he'll have some. I'll have it ready for him.

I better ponder lunch. It takes some thought to cook for these people. Dahlia's a vegetarian and Hugh's lactose intolerant and if Max gets thrown into the mix we can't have fish. That leaves pasta and my repertoire's exhausted.

I sit down at my fake marble table. It looks like a black and white picture of Earth from outer space. It's a replica of the floor at MoMA. Callie gave it to me. When she and Max broke up I got all his stuff.

I sip my coffee. I look around my apartment. I wonder what Hugh will think of my minimalism. My room at the coop was maximalist in extremis. It suited my found objects mood. I never could understand why people threw away perfectly useful stuff, they'd just leave whatever on the street, abandoned chairs, VCRs, old clothes, imperceptibly chipped mirrors. What was the impulse? Disposable society? Recycling? I picked up everything, even things that were obviously damaged. Especially those. They made the best art. They were the most fun to transform.

Hugh loved my room. He'd come over, pick an album, play it over and over till the neighbors complained. I'd inherited 362 LPs from my parents, they'd loved the blues, they'd lounge to spinning vinyl with coffee or wine and me in their laps, I've seen photos, but

Hugh and I mostly listened to Sentimental Walk from Diva. He bought it for me, we'd rented the video like 8 times. We'd listen to that last breathy high piano note and Hugh would stop whatever he was doing, go to my turntable, raise the needle arm, start it again from the beginning. He looked great in the dim green light of the neon tubes that ran through my car crash collages. It made his eyes greener. He knew it too. He basked in it. He sat with his back to the dangling Bay Bridge which was right out my window. I'd sit with my back to him, let him look at me. Let him wonder what I'd be like.

I'm more subtle now. And I don't do car crashes. My new collages are nude selfportraits in Kodacolor. I cut up photos and reassemble them with paint and Elmer's glue. Not a computer. I hate that pixilated flatness, that lack of depth. My pieces have been touched. My fingerprints are on them. My breath. My favorite is I of the Beholder. My head is severed from my body, tethered by a delicate black velvet ribbon tied around my bloodless neck. I'm Manet's Olympia in her own eyes. I'm lying on a silken bed, my torso illuminated with a harsh acrylic spotlight, my breasts are hollowed in places, plump flesh scooped out by chiaroscuro. The rest of the image fades to black, catless.

5 days till my first solo show. I need to work on a

couple of pieces a little while longer. The rest I have to look at. I have the week off which is good and bad. I need to get my show together but I miss my job, miss The Archive, miss the rush of associating with genius. I match works of art to people's needs, magazine and book people, photo editors call, they ask for me, they tell me what they want to illustrate, what they want to portray. I find just the right image. I'm good at that. I have the entire archive in my head, the entire history of art. It makes me a superb artist. That's what I think.

I can't wait for my show. It's not a big deal gallery but I can use the exposure. And the dough. It's times like this I wish I had a real name. Who's gonna buy dismemberment collages from someone named Becky? Dahlia says I should use Beck but it's taken. At my last group show I was Becky S. which made me feel like someone in rehab. Actually I sold a lot. Not just to Dahlia.

I can hear the icecubes jingling in her empty juice-glass. She's coming up the hall. She walks with every inch of her long feet which produces a nice bounce in her stride. And the jingle. Her excellent posture doesn't collapse when she leans against my kitchen wall. Still out she reports. He could sleep all day Dahlia, then what?

Just be patient Beck, what difference will a couple of hours make? Nothing gets me stressed like waiting. Whatever Dahl. This whole thing was your idea in the first place.

Dahlia goes I'm calling Max. She reaches for the phone on the wall behind me but I grab her wrist in motion. Wait a sec Dahlia. Her mouth is the same height as my eyes. I watch it flex into a smile. What's up Beck? I know what you're up to Dahlia, not the details but the gist. You think you do Becky but you don't. I'm still holding her wrist. Beck let me get Max before he leaves or something ok? he absolutely has to be here.

She punches his number which is not on speeddial. I have to sit down. I walk the 3 inches to my livingroom, bring my coffee, slump on the couch. There's only 1 piece of furniture in my minuscule livingroom, a very long vinyl couch in pale pink, smack in the center of the room. I bought it with the money from my last show. Dahlia's money. She bought the collage called Dahlia, Remember When We Lived in Paris? We never lived in Paris. I grafted us into Brassai photos of prostitutes and Carnival dancers, I painted us Phthalo blue, intensely. We looked good that way. That was my Exile Artists period, when I still thought we were making our own Paris on the East River, when I still thought of my friends as artists.

Dahlia. Come sit here with me for a minute. I pat the vinyl next to me. Ok Beck but I'm not gonna tell you yet no matter how charming you are. Don't worry Dahlia, I will not be charming. She laughs and I almost believe whatever she's cooked up will turn out fine. You ok Dahl? Yes Becky. You know you can tell me anything Dahlia. I know. And I will. She just sits there. Looking at me. I twirl my hair, grin at her, say Dahlia remember when we lived in Paris? She smiles. I remember she says, beaming. We sit looking at each other. Dahlia starts wiggling on the vinyl. Oh no you don't Becky, you said you wouldn't be charming. She springs up and goes to wait for Max by my intercom, to muffle it with her wadded sweater so Hugh won't be disturbed. The second Hugh sees Max he'll be disturbed.

I lie down, watch the light through my dirty windows making shapes on the ceiling, wonder what's about to happen, how bad it'll be, how futile to bring them together. I picture Hugh and Max with their hands around Dahlia's throat, me trying to pry them off her. Maybe they'll like each other. Maybe Hugh will shake Max's hand and say No hard feelings. Maybe Max will

karen mckinnon

charm Hugh with his actor's grin and Hugh will excuse Max because who wouldn't fall for that? Yeah sure. Can a man be friends with the man who took his lover away? Or whose lover he took? Can a woman who's not even in the picture anymore destroy all potential for The muffled intercom blare makes Dahlia jump. She pushes buttons, goes I'll be right back Beck, goes to the bathroom. All that orange juice. I get up, go to the door, open it, listen for the hollow echo of Max's footsteps on the stairs, let Max in. He's looking strangely alert. His eyes are shiny, bigger. He has a new facial hair configuration. He has a new one every time I see him. He has a black tuft under his lower lip. He looks deranged. I think he knows this, he goes cleanshaven to auditions. Max is rarely cleanshaven.

Hey Beck, how ya been? Good Max. He brushes by me, kisses me on the cheek but misses a little and nearly gets my ear. The tuft tickles or maybe it's his breath, the rush and tingle of somebody exhaling near that part of my face. Where's Dahl? he wants to know immediately. She's in the bathroom. Oh. Max throws his backpack on the floor by the door like in case he wants to flee. I can't remember the last time we were alone. He's always strange around me. He's edgy, looking all over, at anything but me. Got any coffee Becky? Help yourself Max. He escapes to my kitchen. Go ahead and hide I want to say.

I met Max in New York. I'd been here 2 days. He was working lunch at a sushi restaurant. Mainly he stroked Callie's hair and watched us eat. Callie wouldn't let me leave a tip. She called him Love. He said I'll be home by 4 to help with dinner. We took off, Callie showed me St Mark's, Astor Place. Her New York didn't seem so big, more like she'd traded one Berkeley for another. I thought we were having a great time, walking arm in arm past all the wacko clothes store windows, Callie taking in our reflected selves, flipping her hair noir as she talked to me, admiring her pale arms, her breasts in profile. Then she goes Uh, Becky, I kind of want to be alone for a little while, do you mind? I didn't have anywhere to go so I wandered around the East Village with hurt feelings, bereft and ashamed that I was incapable of holding her attention. I just kept walking, hit Tompkins Square Park, got scared, pictured a grimy smelly guy cutting my throat with the broken glass I was walking on, walked west toward the Bowery, looked for a bookstore, found a cafe. I got coffee and thought up stuff to say at dinner, not lies, just ways of framing my life before New York to seem less lonely. I'd grown up deflecting pity, I knew what I was doing.

I took red wine. Callie kissed me on both cheeks. Twice. Before I even got in the door. Ca va? I don't speak French but that didn't stop her. Whenever I'd see her she'd kiss me on both cheeks twice and say Salut Coco a couple octaves high. Then she'd laugh when all I said was Hi.

We got drunk at dinner. Callie fed us green spaghetti. While I was eating she goes Sorry Becky, I marked you. She licked two fingers, rubbed my cheeks where she'd kissed me. I felt her saliva on my face. I felt the liquid euphoria of her attention. I felt Max looking at me. I felt uncomfortable. I started thinking about the last time I had sex, my head kept hitting the headboard in the Santa Cruz motel room. The relationship was so almost over, like the sex, it didn't seem worth repositioning. I was telling Max and Callie about it, trying to sound like Hugh wasn't why I was in Santa Cruz with someone else, like he wasn't why I was in New York. Callie's hand went over my eyes, she started screaming Oh my god Max. It wasn't the reaction I expected. Her hand was warm. It smelled like sex. I sat there. I heard Max banging pots and pans around and I began to think they were making some surprise or precision dessert. But then I heard Callie say Open the door Max. I pulled her hand away in time to see a mouse run out into the hall.

Callie's face was red and she said It's gone, let's go in the other room. I'd never been in a railroad apartment. Instead of doors there were billowy white curtains separating the rooms. A huge Matisse odalisque in a glass frame hung on a white brick wall. The figure looked like Callie, down to the little red pout of a mouth, the dark straight armpit hair I'd seen Callie flash in public. The place felt French. I was envious of their semiadulterous year in Paris. Which they told me nothing about. I was still more Hugh's friend than theirs.

I peek in at Hugh. He hasn't moved. Just a veinless marble bust sticking out from under my big fat comforter. It's good to have him here. He came for my show. He came for me.

I head for my kitchen. I spy an orange and brown bag on the table. Max embezzles dayold bagels from the Zaro's where he works 2 days. Hugh won't know the difference but Dahlia will balk. I'll just have coffee. I make a fresh pot and hope I have enough half and half to get me to lunch. Half and half's the only way I can drink 7 or 8 cups. That's what I'm up to. That's what it takes to get me up. Making art requires a rev in the blood. I use caffeine like Modigliani used booze. And other substances. And his models. I could never exploit a naked vulnerable person that way. I use myself.

Max goes through my cupboards. He's looking for a plate but he doesn't ask and I don't offer. I hardly ever see him now and there are too many flareups to avoid so I let his rummaging go. Dahlia's back from the bathroom, all attentive to him. She knows his daily life enough to ask relevant questions. How'd that commercial video class work out? Incredible Dahl, and I made an excellent tape to send out. Are you sending it out? Not yet, it's the perennial headshot problem. I've aged out my last ones and I don't have the dough for new ones. Why doesn't Becky take new ones? They both look at me like I'm supposed to defend myself. I guess Dahlia knows what happened.

It started when I left my 30 buck a day room at the Martha Washington Residence for Women. Callie said I could stay with her and Max until I found my own place. She was at work. I was unpacking my suitcases and Max saw Aunt Jane's Rollei. Hey, I thought Callie said you're a painter. I am, I got that and the dough to move here from my dead aunt. He messed with the camera, like he knew how to use it. Know how to use it Max? Sort of. Can I play with it while you unpack? Sure. The instruction book's in the box. Aunt Jane saved everything. Yeah here's a receipt from 1956. Cool.

Max spent an hour trying to get the film loaded. I

offered to help but he said I got it. I was getting ready to go out for mutual groceries when he finally wound the film in right. You get the perseveration award Max. Can I go out with you Becky? I'm just going to the store. Let's go take some pictures first.

He took me up to 11th and C and climbed onto a pile of rubble in a corner of a vacant lot. What do you think? His leather jacket was flapping in the warm wind and I wondered who he thought he was up there. You going for a King of the Hill thing? Sort of. Can you see my face from there? Not if you want the whole hill. The big format camera was meant for landscapes not portraits. I moved closer and closer till I was at the base of the rubble. Broken glass and toilet fixtures and little doll body parts stuck out of the dirt. I looked up at Max. He was undressing. Max are you nuts? what are you doing? Come on, this will be really good. He let his black boots slide down the hill. He draped his clothes over the trash heap. When was your last tetanus shot Max? Shut up and shoot me Becky. I'd like to shoot you Max.

He knew how to work the camera, giving me all his best angles. He had a full beard and his face was super pale by contrast. His body was muscular in a wiry way but soft around the middle. He looked good and I wondered how it would feel to have a penis dangling there

In Transit Slip

above the junk. I was thinking he didn't seem naked, and then it dawned on me that he was turning me into a pornographer of sorts. A crowd was starting to gather behind me. I thought it was funny how they were keeping a hygienic distance.

The Rollei only took 10 to 12 pictures a roll so I was about done. I was looking down into the peep window when the light on Max changed, began to pulse. I looked up at him and he was grabbing his clothes. Run Becky. I did.

I was sitting on their stoop when Max and Callie came home. It was dark. I didn't have a key. Max grinned when he saw me but Callie was pissed. Becky I thought you of all people would have more sense than Max. She grumbled about how much the bail had been. Max said At least you didn't have to pay it for two.

Hugh's bare feet thud up the hall. He turns the corner, groggyfaced, surprised to find a crowd. Dahlia, Max, and I stand up formally. Dahlia goes Hugh this is Max. Dahlia's almost giddy. Hugh looks at me like I can save him. Max shakes Hugh's hand. None of us is talking. I fold my arms and give Dahlia a look. She's ignoring me. It gets very quiet. I can hear the cars screeching down A, my kitchen clock ticking like a cartoon bomb. Hugh says Well. I say Want coffee?

We sit stiffly, listening to each other chew. Even Dahlia's eating the old bagels. She must be nervous. I look each of my friends in the face wondering where this is going. I'm wishing Dahlia would get it over with but she seems intent on her bagel. I can't watch this. I look out the window.

A streak of light flashes across the neighbor's window and we all look. It flashes again. A naked man appears, he's holding a woman, her head draped on his shoulder, her hair cloaks his back when they sway. They reel. She's naked too. They dance away from the window, away from us. We look at each other. Max says Wow, that was beautiful. Hugh goes You mean this doesn't happen all the time in New York? We laugh because he means it. No one's more earnest than Hugh. It's one of his best qualities.

So Hugh, you're some sort of money person, right? high finance? Max is leaning back in his chair, my chair, his chair. I'm wanting him to fall because he's contemptuous of Hugh. Hugh's a CPA. I look at Dahlia whose bright idea this was. Her jaws clamp mechanically as she chews, her eyes are fixed on some lint on Hugh's sweater. Why doesn't she say something already? I raise my eyebrows at her and lean toward the lint, into her line of vision. She's staring. Still. She's having another bagel which makes me nervous.

I can't stand it anymore. I smack my palm on the table. Look, we're all here having this awkward moment because Dahlia's got something mysterious up her sleeve. Hugh's rubbing his eyes and looking thoroughly puzzled. Max sits his chair down on all fours. Dahlia stops chewing. Damn it Becky that is not how I wanted to do this at all. Ouch I say quietly, to hide the sting of her disapproval. Dahlia doesn't snipe very often, I wonder if I actually deserved that. She gets up and starts pacing. We watch her circle the couch a couple of times. She looks like she's stalking something. Ok. Listen. I love you guys. You're my closest friends and I wouldn't have you if it weren't for Callie. Uh oh escapes from Hugh's lips, Max starts pulling on his tuft. Don't freak until you've heard what I have to say ok? We nod. Freaked.

Dahlia comes back to the table. She sits on her leg on the chair. She leans on her elbows on the table. Her arms look as pink as the couch. Her nose looks big with her hair pulled back that tight.

Ok she says finally. I've given this a lot of thought. Hugh, how often do you come? Max snorts at the question and Dahlia puts her hand out and waves it at Max like that will accomplish a personality makeover. To New York she says looking sweetly at Hugh. Oh, well, I come whenever one of you guys has a show basically. Yes, exactly my point. Becky's show. This is the perfect opportunity. For what is what I want to know. My show is my show Dahlia. Yeah Beck but look. Here we are, all of us know each other because of Callie. We're still friends with each other and not with her. Not Hugh and Max I want to say. Hugh clears his throat and goes We're not friends with her for very good reasons. He's eyeing Max evilly. Well, for us Hugh, the 3 of us, we always run into her at our worst possible moments and it's like she sees us at our most pathetic. I'm thinking Yeah, that's happened a couple of times but that doesn't mean we have to do something about it, about her. I go Granted Dahl but what does my show have to do with Look Becky, I want Callie to see that we're better without her, that we're all still friends and thriving. Your show's the perfect thing. We get her an invitation to the opening and she can't resist and we're all there looking incredible and together and she's the one who's out of it for a change.

I can't believe this, and I can't help it I go Dahlia you're not mean enough to think up a suitably vile way to avenge us for all the shit Callie pulled. And I'm not up to murder. Nothing else will satisfy me so why don't we just drop it and get on with our lives. I touch her hand, to soften the blow. Her hand takes mine, holds it, warmly, emphatically. I can't let it go Becky. I can't she almost whispers. She's shaking her head at no one.

Hugh goes Dahlia you're obsessed. He gathers his courage, gathers steam, launches. I have maybe more reason than anyone to hate Callie but I don't because she's seriously fucked up. She never knew her father, and her mother's such a That's no excuse Hugh Dahlia breaks in. We're all victims of something. I don't like where this is going. I'm not about to take part in some Oprahstyle purgefest where we all sit around comparing our traumas. Not Hugh I say brightly, his only trauma is that he was deprived of therapy. Only Max and I laugh and that's the wrong company to be in.

Now no one's laughing, we sit silently, urgesurfing, at least I am. I want to talk about anything but this, but I see Dahlia's distress, and in our little hierarchy of victimization Dahlia reigns. Incest and a dead mother trump 2 dead parents which makes me next. Max and Hugh technically tie for last but Max wins the prize in the 2 screwed parents department. We all know these sad facts about each other, why am I the only one who seems to feel the riptides around our psyches? I mean closure's totally overrated. Besides, delving messes with my imagery, forming the words releases the tension I need to spill onto the canvas. Nope, I want no part of any of this. What good would it do?

Anyway Dahlia pronounces. I don't hate Callie. I just don't think she should get away with everything. She fiddles with the bagel on her plate and looks at Max. He's a terrible actor and I can see he thinks Dahlia's a genius for thinking of this but he doesn't want to commit so he shrugs. Neither of the men can say no to Dahlia so it's gonna be up to me. I'm the one with the most to lose. I can just see us all at the gallery crying and trying to rip each other's eyes out. Just the opening I've been dreaming of.

HUGH

I have no ideas. I've been staring at the same collage for an hour. I painted my Kodacolor nakedness, enhanced my paleness with pink, Dianthus, Ultramarine, Warm, my cheeks and lips and breasts, aroused myself with paint. I am standing, my left arm bent, a black and white object in the palm of my hand. You have to get very close to see that I'm holding a mirror. There's no reflection. Something's wrong. I don't trust myself. I could fuck up.

I'm tempted to abandon this piece, work on another one for a while, give myself a break. I shouldn't. That messes with my impulses, dilutes them. This collage deserves my undivided attention, my moverlove. Like its siblings, this one's frameless. I am beyond containment. I don't believe in it. I imply that in my margins, let my rough edges show. Because I know better than anyone, even Dahlia, that it's impossible to keep a body safe, to enclose it, shelter it, to hem violence, to control the harm that can come to it. That's a reality I'd give anything to undo. Then I could save my parents, lacerated and moaning in the twisted heap of our car, I could save Aunt Jane from the stealth balloon in her artery. But even with art I can't undo the fact that bodies are, ultimately, irreparable. Our junk lasts longer than we do.

Hugh watches me. He doesn't talk. That's the only way he's allowed to stay. The price of annoying me is eviction from my livingroom, my imaginary studio. He picks an album, plays it over and over till I complain. Hugh you're being annoying. He flinches. He picks another album. He comes all this way to be insulted and ignored. He suffers for my art.

I need another coffee. I take what's left, taste the bitterness of the stuff that waits too long to be drunk, try to cut it with half and half, to salvage it, spit it out, like the pattern I've made in my sink, think how infantile Pollock was, stop stalling, get back to work.

I look out of the canvas, direct, unflinching. This is a dare. I must match my subject's gaze with my artist's. I must live up to myself. Any other viewer will have to. I look at my body, see its pleasing curves, follow them with my brush, hope they provoke. Not the obvious. Everyone gets that art is visual seduction, but I'm not after anything that literal. Arousal, yes, unconscious, subliminal. That's what making art does for me, that's what I want my pieces to do to my audience. I look at Hugh to see if it's working.

I watch him get up from my couch. I see him not reacting. He probably thinks my stuff's exhibitionistic, solipsistic. I see him futz with the window gate. See him figure out the lock. See his gorgeous eyes register his breakthrough. Watch him scrunch onto the fire escape, prop his delicate feet on my hibachi.

I pace the room. Not like Dahlia, not stalking some-one I can't get out of my mind. Hugh's right, Dahlia's obsessed. When did that happen? How did I miss it until yesterday? Dahlia's always been so stoic, so careful about what she lets out. I suddenly feel like I don't know her, like I haven't paid enough attention to her. I'm a lousy friend. I feel bad. But I've been there for her. I've been willing. I feel sorry for Dahlia but all I can think is how pissed I am. I can't make a farce of my show, turn it into some ratty Crime and Punishment. I have to do something. I call Dahlia. Hi, it's Dahlia, leave a message. She sounds especially pleased with herself. I hope she hasn't done something stupid. I leave a message. Hey Dahl. Don't do anything ok? About Callie. Call me.

I'm on my couch. I'm lying down. I put my arm over my eyes and try to picture Callie. I remember how purple her blue eyes looked bulging out of red sockets, her face twisted by anger and selfpity. I can barely remember why we were friends. What I remember is the stuff she did to me and anyone else who got close enough. I'd like to stop having to remind everyone of that. I'd like to stop remembering. Can I forget her? What she looks like. How she sounds. Salut Coco. That stays with me.

She said it every time I saw her. Even the first time. She kissed me on both cheeks and I let her in. It was the end of summer and I was still in the house on Haste some of us from the coop had rented. The coop shut down in summer so we found a place near Long Life Veggie Palace, our favorite restaurant. It was cheap. So was our house. A great old Berkeley cottage, with tiny windowpanes, a fireplace we almost needed.

Callie burst in with a bottle of Bordeaux in each hand and a strangely British accent. There she was, big as life, bigger, the intensely blue eyes from Hugh's photos, the inky hair, the tiny mouth, deceptive. Her breasts were in constant motion, you could see them pressed against her shirt. You couldn't help but look at them. She liked for you to look at them. When she'd catch you she'd say Not implants, smiling. She was as tall as Hugh and out of scale in a way I couldn't pinpoint. Hugh followed in her wake. He kissed me on the forehead, said Becky this is Callie. That's all he said all night.

Callie had the floor. She had opinions. The French are egotists she announced. She gauged her effect. We waited for her to elaborate. She goes I mean that in the best possible sense. Then she spent half an hour elaborating, her arms were long and thin and she moved them a lot, to prove her point. The French she was saying are finely tuned instruments, they register every visceral, sensual impulse, every insult, every I escaped to the kitchen, her voice in my ears as I boiled, simmered. The only thing I knew how to make was tomato soup from a can but it was good if you put enough brandy and cumin in it. And hid the cans. We sat down to dinner. Callie positioned herself in front of the only mirror in the room, an ebony oval built into the cabinetry. She included the mirror in the conversation, made meaningful eye contact with herself. With the rest of us too now and then. Haluk and Trevor and Daljit knew Callie from way back. Trevor had a real British accent and he asked Callie where she'd picked up hers. Traveling Love. I took up with a group of Brits after I left Paris. It's contagious Trev. She winked at him and watched herself laugh. Then she looked at the rest of us and watched us watch her laugh. Finally face to face with Callie. I didn't get what was so fascinating about her. She ate my food like a regular human being. She drank a lot of Bordeaux.

I kept looking at Hugh to see whether he saw through her, her pretense, her seemingly infectious, totally distorted view of herself. His arms were folded. His eyes were greyer than green. I couldn't read them. I kicked him under the table. He wouldn't look at me.

Callie did. As the evening slinked on she couldn't take her eyes off me. Except to glance in the mirror. She was sizing me up. She was asking me personal questions. So Becky, Hugh tells me you were in a terrible car accident when you were a kid and you're lucky to be alive. It must have been horrible to lose your parents so young. Are you still having bad dreams about it? She couldn't wait to let me know Hugh had told her everything about me. I kicked Hugh harder under the table. Callie locked her eyes on me. Waited for me to say something. In the tense silence she'd induced in us I kept thinking This is the woman everyone's so charmed by? I was immune to her, or maybe she wasn't sending her vibe my way because this was war. Hugh was our territory. My dinner guests, the first casualties, were starting to shift uncomfortably, waiting for me to come up with something to say to Callie. I was too upset to tell her to mind her own fucking business. I was too nice. I caved. I said You can analyze my dreams over dessert Callie, let's go into the livingroom. I was livid and Hugh knew it. He just sat there. When I brought in the scoops of Ben & Jerry's I saw Callie on the couch whispering to Hugh, nodding maniacally at my picture of him, over on the mantel like a prize, his eyes glinted at us from there. He looked adored. I took the picture.

Where is it now? I must still have it.

I feel the moist pressure of lips. On my forehead. I open my eyes. Hugh is upsidedown, tentative. Want some more coffee? Of course I do. Don't get up Becky, I'll make it. Make it strong Hugh.

He fumbles in the kitchen. I hear coffee beans patter on the floor, clattering silverware in the drawer. I get up. I go to Hugh. He smiles at me, scoops the beans. You're not really gonna invite Callie to your show, are you? Why would I Hugh? I can't think of a single reason to bring her back into our lives, even for one lousy night which, by the way, I should be totally focusing on. Don't worry Becky, I'll take good care of you. I go all mushy. I go all doubtful. I go to the bathroom. I look in the mirror to see why Hugh bothers. It's Day 2 so at least my hair's good. It's long enough to wrap around me, around Hugh. I could just go back, to the kitchen, take him by the shoulders, turn him around, reel him around my livingroom, dance him naked past my windows for my neighbors to enjoy, dance him naked to my bed, hold his face and kiss it. I could. I could look into his eyes, feel the rush that's still between us. He'd look into mine and see how much I love him. How grateful I am he's here, how hopeful I am. How stressed I am. I look like shit.

I walk out of the bathroom. Into the hall. Into the air of dreamy music he's playing. Chet Baker, for me. Imagination is silly you go around willy nilly for example I go around wanting you and yet I can't imagine you'd want me too. He's sentimental. Except with money. He never buys my stuff. And after Dahlia, Hugh can best afford me. I guess I'm not a good investment opportunity, and he doesn't do charity. I turn away. Go to my bedroom, look for that picture of him. It must be in my closet. I have a giant stack of Berkeley stuff. I plow through it. I find my diploma, my student

ID. I used to be blonder. Nicer. I find my box of letters from Callie, the first note she gave me, left under my door at the coop a couple of weeks after that awful first dinner. Just stopped by to pursue our friendship. I'll be up till midnight. Call me. xoxxo Callie. I find my box of pictures. The one of Hugh. The ones of Callie, the one in the Berkeley Rose Garden.

It was my first time alone with her, my first time in the rose garden, rings of trellises tangled in snowy roses tinged with topaz, Jaune Brilliant, Nickel Yellow. I wanted to pick one but I knew I shouldn't. I was early, I rambled down the crescented steps, a palette of rose hues fevered me, the soft petalpinks, the vibrant crimsons. I was dying for a paintbrush or at least a macrolens when Callie appeared. I snapped her as Salut Coco tumbled from her mouth, the kisses to my cheeks. Her lipstick was the shade of a blush. I think she planned it that way, to subliminally incite my compassion, my sympathy. I think she must've been embarrassed about me. She asked me there to pursue our friendship she said, to have a heart to heart. I didn't know if I could trust what was in hers.

She sat me down on one of the curved steps. The scent of sweetness surrounded her, lulled me, falsely and not for long. It took her about 3 seconds to say she wanted to clear the air about Hugh. To learn my intentions. To ask if I was trying to steal him away from her. I said I wasn't. He's my friend Callie, nothing more and nothing less. Her face was processing my answer, picking it apart, for hidden meanings, secret agendas. I had none then, just my feelings, my inloveness with Hugh which she'd sniffed out. How could an artist not fall in love with a man whose name defines color? He was trying to work things out with her that last year at Berkeley, but she'd obviously felt threatened. Why shouldn't she? I was better for Hugh than she was.

Callie said she believed me, said she'd take me at my word. She violated the Berkeley ordinance, picked me a rose the color of her lips, handed it to me, said Good because I like you, we have a lot in common besides Hugh. She doesn't even know me I was thinking as I took the rose from her, pricked my thumb on a fucking thorn, watched a perfect drop of blood bubble there, keeled over. I remember waking up with the heady smell of roses in my lungs, my head in her lap, her fingers combing my hair, her cheeks petalcolored, her lips, smiling. I felt the uneven cement path that circles the garden pebbling my back, watched 3 black birds spiral over us, watched Callie saying You scared the shit out of me Becky, I guess when Hugh said you couldn't stand the sight of blood he knew what he was talking about. I didn't know it was this drastic, was it the accident? I watched her eviscerating my psyche, waiting for my guts to spill. It was bad enough to lose consciousness with an emotional predator, I didn't think I had to let her play my shrink too. I don't talk about that Callie. She stopped combing my hair. You talked about it with Hugh.

Remember this? I hold Hugh's face up to him. He's on the couch. Where I was. Lying down. I should kiss him, not on the forehead. He sits up, unkissed, takes his picture, holds it while he shakes his head. His hair barely moves on his skull, it's way shorter now. His hairline's definitely longer. He waxes nostalgic. Me too. Where'd you take this Becky? Baker Beach. Oh yeah. That's all he says. So fucking guarded. I take the picture away from him.

I sit down at my diningtable, at my collage, stare at the longlost photo, wonder which part of Hugh fits my image, if any, wonder how Hannah Hoch decided which objects belonged together. I go to my bedroom, pull my Hoch book from my shelf, take it back to my table, flip through it, flip out, outdone before I even start. She made perfect beings, perfect, their form, their color, their fierce criticism, their wit. I will never surpass her genius for fusion, never even get near her synthetic virtuosity. I envy her. Hate her. Imitate her. I take my kitchen knife, I do a Hoch, I chop Hugh up, serrate him, take his eye, glue it to the mirror. He's so damn flattered he can't see it's cockeyed, the composition's off. I fucked it up.

Car crashes were easier. I twisted metal. I ran neon tubes like arteries through cracked windshields. I didn't imagine the faces of the victims inside.

Hugh would cringe when I'd start a new one. Why do you need to make another one Becky? Because I do. I'd drag him away from his business books, up to my room to do what I told him. He helped me twist metal, crack windshields. Don't you think you're going too far with this one he said as I spattered red paint. I paused. No Hugh, I don't. What did he know about art? about death? about losing your whole world? He was still wrapped in his privilege blanket, a child compared to me. While I was giving Aunt Jane's doctors permission to turn off her respirator, her brain already dead from the aneurism, Hugh was falling in love. I felt myself wanting something from him, to goad him, to provoke him out of his innocence, his Callie stupor. I went to my window where he was sitting. Hugh I don't think you'd know too far if it bit you on the lip. I bit his lip. He looked at me, put his fingers on his mouth. No Hugh you're not bleeding. But he was wounded. He got up from the window seat. He went to my standardissue coop closet. He took Diva from its shelf and walked it over to the turntable. I knew what was coming. It was his Callie song. It put him in the mood to write to her in Paris. In French. It made him miss her. It made me spatter him with red paint.

I peel Hugh's eye off the tiny mirror to fix the composition, stick it to my finger so I can move it around, move it away from the mirror toward the color of my body, let Hugh's eye hover between mine, see myself as a Triclops, reject the connotations, move the 3rd eye down, make a nipple out of it, know I have another for symmetry but hate the whole idea of some kind of Eve monster with devouring genitalia even if she's devouring with her eyes, don't even bother to try the eye on my crotch, try it in the palm of my hand but that's so messianic, try it floating away from my face but this implies disability, or loss. I want this woman's strength to show.

That's why none of my nudes is accompanied by Psyche. Or a painter in his studio. That's why they're all alone. My selfportraits show the power of a woman who needs no one. In the whole history of art only a few artists have even tried to give the world a glimpse of that kind of power, but they've made ambivalent images at best. There are so many paintings I'd love to revise, to remake, to make mine. Ingres's Chained Angelica with her gemdraped gold locks, erect rosy nipples, distressed face, and bulbous neck, handcuffed to a tree as foam from the sea froths and rises leaving a shark full of menace at her feet. Titian's Danae Receiving the Rain of Gold, her delicate face in pink shadow, her large sturdy limbs comfortable in desire. Cranach's Lucretia, scrawny and lizardeyed and poised to pierce her nipple with a jeweled dagger, her crotch swathed in gossamer. I could do a whole series of Death and the Maiden, revise Wiertz's Beautiful Rosine in profile demurely face to face with a grinning skeleton, Baldung's hairy skeleton that's caught the chubbycheeked, flatbosomed, slumpshouldered young woman by the hair while he ogles her finely detailed pubis.

Hugh gets up from the couch, goes I'm gonna take a shower Becky. I go Ok. I watch him walk away from me, see his saggy chinos from the back, wonder if he ever goes to the gym, wonder how many hours a week he sits around, wonder what his body looks like in the shower.

He's really changed. Time and Callie wore him thin. In a few years he'll be all CPA. Not that he's not neurotic, just not in the right way. His parents were good to him, sent him hiking in the Pyrenees instead of to a shrink. He's probably better off. Everyone I know is overanalyzed, pseudoinsightful. Unlike Hugh.

He was so damn normal. At Berkeley. In his sweater. He had this sweater. The one he wore to Baker Beach. I'd packed a picnicbasket. Cabernet and carrot sticks. Sourdough, salami. Hugh called me Yogi so I had no choice, I called him Boo Boo. It seemed less ridiculous the more wine we drank. I took his picture. The sun went down. We built a fire. He'd brought lighter fluid. I said that was cheating. He said Give me a break Yogi, I'm no boy scout. I thought he was. So fucking loyal, Boo Boo, always prepared.

We weren't saying much. It was freezing. He goes We should leave, I'll drive you by Grace Slick's house, it's right up there. He pointed behind us. I go Great. We didn't leave. We listened to the water, the buzzsaw traffic on the Golden Gate Bridge. He got a blanket from the trunk of his car. He had this Volvo. It was boxy. Dark green, like his sweater. He held one end of the blanket and I held the other, we wrapped it around us, huddled together. I poked the fire with a twisted stick. We hadn't scrounged much driftwood. It was burning out, I jammed the stick into the fire.

It was cold again. I put my hand on his chest, to

touch his sweater. Do you have another layer under this? I patted the sweater. It felt thin. He goes Just a tshirt. I put his hand on my chest. He choked out You? I said Same. I held his hand there, I moved it down, I leaned to kiss him. He cleared his throat, said We should leave.

He almost loved me then. Till Callie's letter came. I was doing switchboard duty. It was Saturday so the board was berserk and I got bonus coop points which meant I could get a better room soon. Hugh brought me my mail. He looked at his. He waved his French postage at me. He could be snobby. He sniffed his letter. He tore it open. He read a few lines, flushed. I plugged a call through. Hugh disappeared.

When I saw him at dinner in the asylumstyle coop diningroom he said Hi, stabbed at his babaganoush. Every now and then he'd mumble something in French. It wasn't sacre bleu so I had no idea what the hell he was saying but he looked so embarrassed. He left the table. I did too, followed him downstairs, into his room. It was dark. He hit the lightswitch, zapped his CD player, hit the lightswitch again. Josephine Baker's voice rippled the dark. I pulled a cord, raised the windowshade, saw the moon over Alcatraz. I wanted Hugh to come to the window, I wanted Hugh. I turned to look at him, watched him sitting on his bed, fluffing his pillow, hugging it. She's having an affair. Some guy named Max. That's all he said.

Now he's in my livingroom, cockeyed. Being my friend. Having wanted me, then not wanting me on the rebound, then wanting me long distance, when I was with someone else, now here. He isn't as curious as he used to be, he doesn't question the why of me anymore. Why doesn't he ask me what I want from him, what I need, who I am all at once, what my art is. I wish I could just The phone rings. It's Dahlia. Hi Dahl, so what's happening? I refuse to discuss this on the phone Becky, without the others. Hugh's right here Dahlia. No conference calls Beck. This is too important. So why don't you just come over. I have an appointment with my herbalist. Oh. Anyway Max is at work. He gets off at 8. We'll meet you at The Woid.

I have to get out of here. Away from my undone pieces which are scaring me, they're demanding and I'm not up to them now. I'm going out for a while! I yell at Hugh and quickly shut my door behind me. My stomach's roiling, I need a walk, fresh air, I need an infusion I realize as I pass the junkie on D who has the shakes. It's the end of the month and her check won't come for days. She looks like hell, hair all matted, skinny and rocking herself. I pop into the deli, pick out something I think she'll like, get myself a dreaded delicoffee, hand the junkie a sandwich, a beer in a bag. She gives me a look like Well if that's the best you can do. I give her my coffee. I go back inside, get another for me. Sip it on the crosstown bus, the uptown bus, take my time, kill it, anything to avoid selfexamination. Analysis smothers art.

There's no better fix than MoMA. I love its clean walls, its garden calm with sculpture, its Planet Earth floor. I flash on my diningtable, see the paint tubes scattered and spent, hope this pilgrimage will shift my perspective, feel my pulse speed as I move through the line of weekday museumfans. I've forged the date on my ancient Art Students League ID like 6 or 7 times, it usually works but you never know, one of these cashiers could be taking classes, know I'm a fake. I lay it down with my cash, hold my breath, don't look at the guy, play it cool, look at him all of a sudden, smile. It works. I'm in.

My first stop, always, the temp space, the one for emerging artists, where my work should be, where the pet of my collage class showed last year. That so set me back. I mean she was good. But I was the Still Life pet.

The Life Drawing pet. I worked my way up the rungs of genre. Pet status just came my way. I didn't gloat. Why should I? I wasn't doing it for that. I just did my work. But then Callie convinced me to go to therapy. It totally screwed my collages. I lost focus, lost control. I've got it back now. I'm getting there. I'll get into this precious little room. Someday. Soon. I think. I hope. I peek in at the installation littering the floor, all aluminum and plexi. Form and texture just don't do it for me. Anyone can do geometry and decorate it. I like people.

I take the escalator to 2. Off the escalator I take a shortcut through Cezanne, past Matisse's bronze backs, past his gorgeous red studio I dream of having, to his Odalisque with a Tambourine. I plant myself in front of her, claim her, make the scattered crowd go around me to see her. She is hazyfaced, smearlipped, hoehanded, her voluminous body pops out of a flattened background of smudged wallcovering, brown shutters, billowing white curtains, snagged, red tambourine like a settee pillow, bloodhued floor. The tension in her body would've been a hard pose to hold. I forget who she was for real. I don't need to know. I know her as she really is. She is the one with the raven hair, the one with the little mouth, the one who looks like she would tell you things you don't want to know.

Like that Hugh was a better lover than Max. He tried harder. When she confided this to me I was aghast, then flattered, she wanted me to be her friend, she was sharing Max with me, giving me ammo I could use against her with Hugh if I wanted. Callie made herself vulnerable. Oh Becky she'd say, I wish I could be as sure of myself as you are. I liked her for it. And I never did tell Hugh what she'd divulged. It might've kept them together, he might've tried even harder with her. She'd come back from Paris to finish school, to make it work with Hugh. They lived together that last year, Hugh forgave her for the affair, the pushover. But he never spoke French to her again. One day I was at Cafe Med, reading The AntiAesthetic over my bottomless coffeecup. I was trying to grasp how modernism could be exceeded, which seemed to be what Hal Foster thought was the imperative of vital art. I liked the idea that the modern myths of progress and mastery had eroded, I was free to make my own myths, or at least I should've been, but I was still stuck on car crashes, and I wasn't getting how I was supposed to break with an art history that valued crisis when crisis was all I knew. I was trying to write a paper about it there in the bluewalled Berkeley institution. I was sleepdeprived, I couldn't focus. I needed more coffee. I was trying to get the attention of the homelesslooking waiter when I heard Callie's laugh, turned to look for her, saw her in the corner with a longsideburned man, heard them speaking French. Then I saw them kiss. I knew he must be Max. I knew what to do. I wadded up my stuff, slithered outside, found a payphone, dialed Hugh. I think there's something you should see. At Cafe Med. Now.

I thought that would be the end of me and Callie, I mean it was the end of Hugh and Callie. But no, from then on Callie took me seriously, as a friend, really wanted me as one, she said so, so easily. That was when she chose me. Becky we have a lot in common besides Hugh. I like you she said, you go after what you want. She knew I knew she'd continued to cheat with Max. I knew she knew I'd sicked Hugh on their little rendezvous. We were even. Equals. We'd done each other a favor really. I had a chance with Hugh finally and their breakup meant I'd freed her to go live with Max who'd just moved to New York. I'd freed her to pursue intensity not safety. Those were her poles and I was the one who showed her that. I changed her. I saw through her and I liked her anyway.

And she taught me things. She won me. Not the

way she won the others. Not in latenight conversations after a breakup or any of the usual scaffolding of friendship. I apprenticed myself to Callie. She taught me how to get what I want. The night before she left Berkeley we went to Blakes, sat upstairs in the Bridge of Sighs booth, watched the guys come in below us. Him she pointed. Him? Yeah, the one with the goatee. Which one with the goatee? The one with the goatee and the blue anorak. Yeah Callie, I see him. Know how I'd seduce him? I shook my head, leaned closer to her. I'd brush by him, let him smell me. Call him by whatever name popped into my head. He'd go No, it's Mike. I'd go You sure? He'd laugh and then I'd ask him what he's drinking. He'd say Beer no doubt. I'd say No, you have to taste this. And I'd buy him a Borneo Fogcutter and he'd take a sip and cough because it's bloody strong. When he coughs I step back so he can get a really good look at me, at all of me. That's 3 of his senses that belong to me. The last 2 are the most important Becky. First I'll touch the sleeve of his anorak which will make him touch my sleeve. When he does I'll lean toward his ear and sigh so he'll know how he might make me sound, then I'll call him by his real name and say Why don't we get on a plane to Budapest, I know a great little restaurant that's open all night.

Callie could've gone on like that. So could I, listening to how she could size up a stranger. Me. She got me, made me feel how good I was, how strong. Becky she said. Max called me from the East Village. He found us a railroad flat. Tomorrow I get some dough out of my mom and I'm gone. Just like that? Yep, just like And then she swallowed her martini and everything else she was ready to be done with. And if you stay here Becky you're gonna stay as small as this hippie college town. You're too big for this place, your talent is. Come visit us, you'll see what New York's like. Everything matters there.

I move against the current of artgawkers, let the foreign languages waft over me like perfume, skip Picasso who the crowd fawns over mindlessly, dwell on Brancusi's stone and hacked wood, dis his metal, pass the Ernst I once paid homage to, his Rendezvous of Friends/The Friends Become Flowers became my Rendezvous of Max's Friends, I photocollaged us all into roses, no mean feat such transformation. I did it seamlessly.

I move to the Kahlo with mirrors, the one with the winged eyebrows, the furry lip, the ribbon trying to escape the peltshaped hair. Her symbolism eludes me, makes me think there's a right answer I can't fathom for the cracked leaves, the furry phallic cacti behind her, the monkeychild she holds. Her face is blemished with clumps of paint, a dot sits on the tip of her nose like makeup applied without a mirror. She stares, immobile, not into my eyes but at my shoulder. Why did she do that? Why did she render her powerful gaze oblique? Why couldn't she look directly at herself? That can't be it. I think she was doing the viewer a favor. I think it proves her compassion. I think it's the frame of cracked mirror that makes me anxious, it insists you see your cracked self in the portrait. I want to do that without mirrors.

I know what I want. My ritual visit is doing what I wanted. I turn away from my new touchstone Kahlo, almost crash into a glass case, laugh at myself for nearly having destroyed its sacred contents, a metronome with a cutout eye on its ticker, Man Ray's Indestructible Object, the metaphor for me.

I catch the F, head downtown, where I belong. The subway stinks, it has a human smell that makes me anxious. My gut feels tight and tense. I break the code and look my fellow passengers in the eye, a girl with magenta hair and pierced cheek, an old lady hunched and wearing too many kinds of plaid. I put them on edge, still processing Kahlo's gaze I guess, wishing I knew how to reveal myself in my work, to make others see themselves in me. I'm overthinking it, my impulse to work is on the verge of totally fizzing. I picture myself as a glass of flat champagne on my table next to Hugh's cutout eye. Fuck. I've lost it again. I've ruined myself.

Maybe steam would relax me, free me from myself, free me to work. Maybe it's Ladies' Day at the Russian & Turkish Baths. Or at least Coed Day. It has to be. I buy a cheapo towel on my way downtown, don't dare go home to get one, don't dare see my work now, head to 10th, climb the steep stoop up, hesitate at the door, read the sign. Good, it's still Coed Day, that hasn't changed. I hate change. The kind you don't inflict. I go to the desk, flash my towel, leave my cash, strip in the changing room, stuff my hair into a nest. It's quiet. Calm. Rushhour relaxation happens post 9 to 5. I have the steam to myself. I recycle my own anxiety, no neurosis osmosis from strangers.

Or friends. Callie and I used to come here on Ladies' Days. Oh why can't I go anywhere without feeling her presence? Or is it her absence I'm feeling? I try to remove her from the premises, from my memory which associates her way too often with too many things. I try to empty my mind, relax into the heat and thick moisture, breathe it in, linger in it. I feel afraid, alone. I douse myself with water, cool my burning face, immerse my emptiness, hose down my pileup of loss and wanting and fear.

I used to feel so revived by this place. We'd come out of the steam, glowing, stop at the A & P for a gallon of H_2O, drag ourselves to my place, collapse on my bed. I'd lie there a minute, listening to our breathing slow, drag myself up, out to my stereo, put Bessie Smith on my turntable, go back to my bed, fall on it, feel Callie bounce with my reverberation, drift, float, feel lucky to be alive. She'd lie there, languorously, her eyes half closed, her fingers combing my hair, quiet till Bessie sang I Want Every Bit of It. Callie'd sing along, a slow rumble, building, then at the top of her lungs she'd blast at the ceiling I want every bit of it or none at all cause I don't like it secondhand I want all your kisses or none at all Give me lots of candy Honey love is grand It was like she was alone, and her ease was the true proof of our friendship, that's what I thought. Oh why couldn't Callie always be the dream we all kept having. Why couldn't it last? Nothing ever does.

I look at my body, amazed that I have devised such

horrible things to do to it with scissors and paint and glue. I'm not enacting masochistic fantasies or internalizing a hostile male gaze or cutting up the mother who abandoned me, no Freudian, feminist, PoMo analysis covers what I'm doing. I just want to reorder my idea of who I am, what art is, what beauty is. The last time we ever came here Callie looked frankly at my body, told me I was lovely, like she'd just noticed me. She told me she envied the beauty of my proportions, she told me she wished she didn't, she cried. She said she knew that her attractiveness lay in how she orchestrated people's impressions of her, how she calibrated what use they could put her to and then filled their need. I felt bad for her, embarrassed, wished how I looked wouldn't come between us. I told her about how Kant might've said I was beautiful but he would've called her sublime. He would've. It didn't occur to me she'd actually go to the library and read him, find the words horror, dread, and melancholy, call me up in a rage. I tried to explain that beauty was L I T E and the sublime so much more interesting and worthwhile. She didn't buy it. She hung up on me, wounded. She looked at me differently after that. She began to look at how everyone else looked at me.

Fred was really someone I could've lasted with, a great guy, a great lover. I wasn't sure how much I was into him when he first asked me out so I suggested we double with Callie and that guitarist she was seeing. Santo. We went to Time, had a great one, Callie made a great impression, she could just make you feel so amazingly interesting, and Fred was liking it at first but then in the middle of dinner he just stopped slurping it up. Later he told me he'd all of a sudden felt overwhelmed by her, he goes She could kill you with kindness. Fred started angling to get away from them, Santo was doing likewise with us, but Callie wasn't having any of it. She kept coming up with stuff we all could do together after dinner, I thought she was trying to signal me that something had gone wrong with Santo, although I couldn't see what. So I told Fred I thought Callie needed me, that I'd call him the next day, date over. Callie and I were on our way to her place and I was like So what happened with Santo? She goes What are you talking about, I thought you wanted out of Fred. I really believed her and we laughed about it and then I told Fred and we laughed about it.

Fred was like that. He got what it was like to be me. He knew how to get inside me. He was working on his PhD, in Cinema, his mom and dad were professors, of philosophy and music, in that order. I think. He spent a lot of time with them. After that first date gone wrong he started calling me, every day, no will he or won't he games, no if I fall for him he'll lose interest instantly. He'd call me, tell me he was thinking about me, tell me about his family outings, little glimpses of something I could be part of. He'd want to know what I was doing. Usually I was at work, surrounded by all the other researchers, I had to pretend he was a magazine editor. So what kind of image did you have in mind Fred? Well Becky I was picturing you at my parents' country place. There's this lake where we swim all summer and I thought you might like to row me around it. Um hmm. Is that for a cover? No, that particular image is for between covers, you all muscular from the rowing, with the sun shining down on your pretty head, that's definitely an image I curl up with when I hit the pillow lately. I could pull some Goyas for you, Saturn Eating His Son, that might be right for illustrating the sort of greed you're talking about. So when can I see you? he said, greedily.

But when Fred and I really got together Callie started in for real. She was over one day and he called while I was in the shower and she just happened to forget to give me the message and he was mad for like 2 days thinking

I was trying to blow him off. So he hadn't called me which pissed me off. Then we made up but then when the 3 of us got together, and that happened way too often, she'd say stuff about me, in front of me, in this hilarious but demeaning way. When Becky gets tired doesn't she look like Harpo Marx? Then she started calling him, sort of crying on his shoulder about her failed romance with his roommate, but he said she'd always get around to telling him how manipulative I was and he hadn't known me that long and even though he believed me more than her he still started to see what I was doing or saying along the lines of what Callie had told him. She totally poisoned his idea of me. I confronted her about it but she goes Becky I never said that to Fred, what I said was and then she'd tell me some good version of what she'd said. So there I was beginning to believe it was Fred who was wacked.

The last straw was Christmas. Callie wasn't good at holidays. She stopped by my place when she knew Fred was over and she had presents for us. Mine was like some French baking dish or something, she was always trying to teach me to cook. Then Fred, who was already weirded out about Callie for too many reasons, not to mention that he didn't have anything for her, he opened his pretty little package. Silk underwear. By that point I was so paranoid I figured either Callie was trying to tell Fred that I didn't think he was sexy, which I didn't but that was before we slept together, or this was Callie's way of telling me they were sleeping together, which I now realize is an insult to Fred.

Nothing was ever what it was supposed to be with her, so you had to be on top of her mood, had to look out for the scorpion in the gift box, try to see what she was really trying to get from you, how she would extract it from you whether you knew it or not. It was exhausting, I couldn't deal. Fred and I tried to patch things up after that but Callie had just ruined whatever had been good between us and it was totally over. Callie sent me these long, tortured letters trying to find out why I was being so cold, saying I owed it to our friendship to hear her out about Fred, still sort of implying there was something between them that needed explaining when she was the problem. Callie was a problem. That reality finally hit me. Hugh's reality.

I better get back to him, he's been waiting around for me for hours. Years maybe. I wrap my towel around me, feel thin but not light, feel shriveled, feel weak.

I turn in my locker key, head toward home spent,

needing a nap. I picture myself flopping on my bed, blasting my stereo, listening to Bessie Smith, hearing Callie give that song all she's got.

It's 8:35. Hugh and I snagged a great table far from the giant Bose speakers that will gurgle poetry at 9. For now it's Jimi Hendrix wailing, impossible to turn into background. Great place for a chat. Hugh's sipping a Pinch on ice. I'm sucking air through the straw in what was a luscious Baileys and coffee. I think I'll have another.

There's Dahlia waltzing in late. She waves at me like no big. Then she goes to talk to some stringy guy at the bar. The bartender joins them. Dahlia knows him. She knows everyone, she comes here all the time. How can someone who doesn't even drink coffee be a regular at a coffeehouse? She waves at the guy setting up the mike.

Hugh goes I'll get you a refill. Thanks Hugh. Make it I know he says, make it strong. He joins Dahlia and her uncoffeeklatsch at the bar. I watch them. See how Hugh stands so close to her. See her stick her hand into what's left of his hair, rub his head. See him love being touched, noticed. See how needy he is. How Dahlia caresses him with attention. How his eyes practically roll

Karen McKinnon

back in his head with it. I'm thinking I have to leave ASAP to fix See Through, that's what I'll call it, the piece I fucked up. I know what to do. I know what it is. The naked I, defenseless, can't exist without being watched.

Max walks in squinting. He stops inside the door like he's walking into daylight and he has to let his eyes adjust. Too vain for glasses. He sees Dahlia, moves toward her, scans the room, sees me. He stops. He looks both ways. He comes to me.

He scrapes his chair my way, drapes a leather sleeve over my shoulder, whispers hotly in my ear Becky don't say anything, let me talk. Shoot Max. He pauses. I made him remember. We haven't made this joke for ages. It irked Callie. Like the word bail. Max is laughing. A scatty laugh. His tuft is gone. Do you have an audition Max? Yeah, how'd you know? Lucky guess. I'll tell you all about it in a sec Becky but I wanna tell you something serious. Serious? Serious. Don't oppose Dahlia on the Callie thing ok? Max I am not going to let Dahlia Trust me Becky? please just trust me and let her do this weird thing. What the hell is my show some charity event? Keep it down Becky here comes Dahlia. I'm gonna get a drink. Want anything? Yeah. A Baileys and coffee, here's some dough. It's on me Becky.

I'd like it to be on you Max. I picture splashing a scald-ing not tepid glass of the delicious stuff all over his pre-cious face. I lick it off while we wait for EMS to arrive. They arrive, put him on a stretcher, rush him to the Cor-nell burn unit where they discover that his wounds have miraculously healed.

See, I have my own revenge fantasies Dahlia, but I don't have to act them out. Dahlia finally makes her way to me. She swooshes into the chair next to mine, her long sheer skirt rustles when she jackknifes her leg, sits on it. I can smell her perfume. Hi Beck, ready? For what is what I want to know. I am if you are Dahl. Yep. Just waiting for the boys. Max and Hugh serpentine toward us, each holding his own drink and one for me. Things are looking up.

Hugh wants to know how the coffeehouse got its name. It's The Word with a New York accent right? Max rolls his eyes like Hugh's an ignoramus. It's a Vien-nese coffeehouse Hugh. Sound it out. Hugh gives it a try. The Void he says rolling his eyes, that's awfully exis-tential Max. Awfully Max says, doing his best Malkovich sneer. Things are not looking up. I have a stomachache. I want to go home.

Dahlia goes Knock it off you guys. You see? she looks at me. This is what I mean. She looks at them.

You're both perfectly wonderful but you hate each other's guts because of Callie. It's time to put her in the past where she belongs. I go Look Dahl, she is in the past for most of us. That came out meaner than I meant. And louder. The people at the tables near us are staring. We are not cool. We can be heard fighting over the gush of cappuccino machines, over the scrape of spoons in cups, over the rattle of strange voices, over Callie. I lean onto our table, whisper I don't need some group healing exorcism to be over Callie. If you do, fine, but do it on your own time, not at my show.

Dahlia's eyes are wet. She's going to cry. I look at Hugh whose hand's on top of Dahlia's on her lap. Max is glaring at me. What's the big deal Becky? can't you see Dahlia's just trying to help? I know he's right but this whole thing's just getting totally blown out of proportion. I so hate this. Max is looking at me, deadly. Don't be such a hardass Becky. My hand is on my full glass. Just a flick of my wrist and he'd be so sorry he said that. I should at least slap him. I push away from the table. Max goes It's not gonna wreck your sacrosanct show to have Callie there, if she even comes. I'm shocked. I didn't know sacrosanct was in Max's vocabulary. I get up. Hugh and Dahlia are watching me, mute, eyes overbig. Max is rabid. He gets up. Can't you ever just once see someone else's side of things Becky? Shut up Max. That bald face of yours would really sting if I slapped it. Try it Becky. Stop it! Dahlia begs. Loudly.

I look around, scan the tables around us, wonder what Callie would think of us now, search faces, eyes, lips, ears holding back hair, not Callie's, close my eyes, lose my balance a little, listen for her laugh, half wanting her to be there, revved, really hoping. I open my eyes, look at my friends looking up at me, seeing my weakness, my need. Selfloathing hits me like a wave of nausea. Dahlia's right about us. We haven't moved on. We're not over Callie. I'm not.

I sit back down. Max is drilling into me with his eyes. I'd still like to slap him but now I know that's so residual. Something Callie would do. Did do.

We'd gone to Elaine's. Because of Woody Allen. He was the reason I'd moved to New York in the first place. I thought I'd have a great apartment like his. And friends. I was still staying at Max and Callie's and we'd been exploring Manhattan, Woody's city, my city. We shopped at Dean & DeLuca, went rowing in Central Park. And now Elaine's. We got a table. Over salad Max whispered something to Callie and her face flushed but she smiled at me, said Max it's not polite to tell secrets, tell Becky what you said or I will. Max looked at

Callie, pleaded with her with his eyebrows, got nowhere, looked at me, goes Uh, I said Look sweetheart, our little girl's not wearing a bra. I hadn't realized it was so obvious. Who would notice my breasts when Callie's were in the vicinity? I must've turned red, betrayed my bourgie morality. Callie goes Don't be selfconscious about it Becky. She started wiggling around in her sweater, pulling her long arms out of their sleeves, wiggling some more until a bra appeared in one of her hands. She draped it over the table and put her arms back in her sleeves. There, now you're not alone. Callie would always join me, in anything.

Callie and Max were finishing their argument. I was finishing my salad. They shut up when a busboy came over to clear away our plates. He left the bra. We sat there awkwardly for eons, looking around the room at the checkered tablecloths, at the crowd clotting at the bar, at anything but the bra. Finally Max exploded. Put the goddamn bra away Callie. Callie leaned back and with all her strength smacked her hand across Max's cheek. Don't you ever tell me what to do.

Max is good at telling people what to do, but I will not be manipulated. But he so pisses me off that I would be unkind to Dahlia just to spite him. Max has his arms folded so tight his muscles look big. Hugh is sitting too still, like moving constitutes an opinion. Dahlia wipes the back of her hand across her nose. I feel ill. Really tense. Nauseous. I really want to go home but I can't leave this much unfinished business.

We're ready to start gurgles the speaker. Great. Now we get to sit and stew while some poet spills his metaphoric guts. Tonight The Woid is proud to present a wonderful poet, Peter Nickowitz. Peter will read some of his published poetry and also treat us to some new work. A boyish boy with stiff hair and Bambi's eyes walks up to the microphone. He's holding some magazine I've never heard of with a couple of pages rolled back and some loose pieces of paper. He clears his throat, smiles, looks around the room, clears his throat again. Cartography after 6 months. The bathroom faucet is a metronome it clocks and wastes the delayed day the boundless anticipation of a hotel room Visiting you is like seeing Israel it might as well have been a second home a single bold blink of a Monarch's wing If I were smarter I'd chart every minutia your face drawn leaner your pale skin defiant against sun glows like the night air in winter In minutes we enter an airport embrace you become holy the dusting of freckles across your nose I can't believe this, everything, even this poet's freckled map of reverence, returns me to Callie. This guy's got his own Callie, this sweet poet boy. He's so open, so tender as he reads. Not plotting some stupid retaliation. He speaks his want so clearly, the perfect antidote to these people, my friends, the egomaniac schemers I'm here with. I look at Dahlia and Max. What kind of artists are they? they're barely paying attention, halfheartedly turned toward the stage, Hugh too, they're all stuck in their own muddled selfinterest, in their unthinking heads. And mine's so fuzzy all I can think of is Callie. I mean I have work to do. I have a show to put up. They don't even seem to think that's important, they're so unbelievably selfish. They never ask me how it's going. Like my work doesn't matter. Maybe they think my collages suck. Maybe they do suck. They're about nothing, about my inconsequential art historical reinterpretations, about my inconsequential personal preoccupations which couldn't seem more artificially preserved than they do right now. I don't deserve a solo show.

The waiter at the next table whispers Ready for dinner? The word dinner ignites a fuse deep inside my stomach. I picture what I should've eaten, I picture the day's actual intake. I picture a generic coffeepot sitting on its industrial warmer, the dregs simmer acidly. I taste my sour saliva. I whisper to Dahlia I'll be right back. I go to the bathroom. Not discreetly. I feel so bad.

I feel even worse when I see my fluorescent reflection. I'm all unfocused. I don't look like me. I'm not the naked I constantly under surveillance. I'm the eye trapped inside the mirror's reflection that can't see out of it, and that's what the naked I sees. Selfportrait.

Who the fuck am I kidding. If I made a selfportrait right this second it would be vomit on the flaky mirror. I'd do a Callie when Hugh ended it finally. She stumbled up the stairs to my room in the coop saying Becky I didn't know who else to call, psychobabbling about abandonment, about her truant father, about pushing men away, always, how her mother couldn't forgive her for blossoming, for becoming sexual, for becoming a woman and stiffening the competition, so to speak, how Callie was so afraid, of being alone, of her mother's retaliations. She turned so white suddenly, turned away from me, ran to my bathroom. I ran after her, smelled the sour odor of her selfindulgence before I could turn on the light, found the switch, saw the streaks of her regurgitation on my mirror.

I buckle, hit my forehead on the sink, veer toward the toilet. My aim is good. I flush. I need air. I open the door. Dahlia's standing there. She's worried. She's coming in. She hugs me, holds my hair out of the toilet when I resume my retching. I'm ok Dahlia. Yeah, you look fantastic. I get up, she holds me steady. I look up into her lovable eyes. She smiles. She cleans me up. Wipes my hot face with a wet papertowel. You'll be ok Becky. Yep. Now I will.

She opens the door for me. A rush of cool air revives me a little. I see Hugh leaning against the wall near the phone. He's sort of folded into himself. He looks up when we walk out. How're you feeling Becky? I'm feeling Viennese Hugh. Huh? It's not just that Hugh's a CPA. He's so earnest sometimes I want to slap him. Why would such a warm, smart man waste his talents hoarding money for people who already have enough. I wanted him to run an arts foundation. Dahlia goes Come on, I'll get a cab. She's pulling me by the hand, around the tables at the back of the cafe. The poet's still reading, his soft deep voice buoys me out the door. I lean against Hugh while Dahlia fends. Where's Max? He thought it would be better if he left. How perceptive.

I don't throw up in the cab. I am triumphant. We don't have too far to go and there's so much traffic we don't move too fast. I sit with my nose out the window like a dog. Dahlia and Hugh are chatting away. I begin to wonder if they've come to some agreement behind my back but at the moment I can't bring myself to really care. I just want to go home, down some aspirin, eat some toothpaste, go to bed.

We pull up to my building. Dahlia leans over Hugh and kisses my cheek. Once. Sleep it off Becky. I'll call you in the morning. Not too early Dahlia. Duh Beck. I pop open the door and fall out of the taxi. Hugh pulls me up and I hear Dahlia laugh. Get it together Becky.

Hugh walks me past the frontdoor of my building. You missed Hugh. I know Becky. Let's walk you around some, you'll feel better. I doubt it. I'm pretty shaky, pretty feeble, pretty sure I won't make it to the end of my block, that my body will give up no matter what Hugh says. But he's right. I start to get my legs back. I didn't even drink that much Hugh. You drank enough. You and Max. He did a couple shots of tequila at the bar. He's an asshole Hugh. No argument from me Becky. I look up into his sage eyes, ask How's it been for you being with him? He pauses, we stop walking, he's still holding me. It's funny how often I've imagined him, you know? what he must be like and why Callie left me for him. I'd always hoped it was just bad luck, you know, timing, that they got together in Paris because it was Paris. But now that I've spent a little time with him, seen him in action, especially with you tonight, I see how inevitable they were. Too true Hugh. Max is a blowhard badboy, just what Callie would mistake for passion. Yeah, Callie always wanted someone who could match her intensity. I sure didn't. You're just intense in a subtler way Hugh. I hold his hand, feel his fingers in mine, soft and uncertain. I hold on.

He starts us up walking again. We circle the block not talking. He gives me a tic tac. I rest my head on his shoulder. I look at the creamy part of his neck where his beard ends. I press the slope of my nose into it. I inhale. He smells like my soap. I kiss the spot, feel its warm softness on my lips. A new favorite part of Hugh.

Are you ready Becky? For what Hugh? He smiles. Let's go up.

In the elevator I go back to the spot. I kiss it. I lick it. I bite his ear, breathe into it. The elevator stops and the doors slide open. I unbuckle my backpack, feel for my keys, let us in.

We stammer toward my bed. I'm swooning a little. Hugh is being his gentle inert self. We stand there. It's dark. The streetlight through my Venetian blinds slats Hugh's tender face. His eyes fill the frame. His nose is gone. His lips, centered in a horizontal bar, are no longer pink. In the dark everything is black and white.

I take Hugh's hand. He holds mine in both of his. He gets down on his knees. He hugs my legs. I feel his breath through my skirt. I fall backwards, onto my elbows, my legs splay inelegantly. I raise my skirt, Hugh pushes it off over my head. Like how I was undressed as a kid. Just when you think you know all your memories a stray one sneaks up on you. Hugh touches my underwear, puts his palm on the cotton. Which ones am I wearing? I look down and see a band of Hugh's hair. Where it's still thick. I can't see my panties. Oh well. It's only Hugh. My Hugh.

He doesn't even try to pull my underwear over my boots which zip all the way up to my knees in an obvious way but he doesn't take them off me either. He's using his thumb to stretch my panties to one side. He opens his mouth, breathes on me like I'm a windowpane. He's moving deliberately. Like he's imagined this a thousand times. For once he knows what he wants. He puts his mouth on me. I feel his lips kissing me. I feel his tongue begin to moisten me. I close my eyes. How long I've waited for this. How long I've wanted Hugh, wondered what he'd do to me, how he'd make me feel. How many times I've imagined him. How many men I've imagined were him. How many? I open my eyes, tense up, worry for Hugh. Maybe I should go get some Saran

Wrap Hugh. Some what? You know, I gave blood last year but I haven't been tested since Steve and I'm just thinking Where is it Becky? In the second drawer from the top on the left. I'll be right back.

The light scans him as he stands up, leaves me. I unzip, undress. I can hear the kitchen drawer opening, the slide of the box being drawn out of it. Hugh's footsteps sound efficient. They arrive. Becky, you only have foil. What? There's only one box in the drawer and it's foil. Fuck it. Let's just switch gears and use a condom. I don't have any Becky, do you? I yank on the drawer of my nightstand, rustle around in it with my hand. Nothing. Could the Saran Wrap be anywhere else? No, that's my wrapdrawer.

He sits on the foot of my bed. Is there a drugstore nearby? I picture him over on B with the junkies, know they'll see dollar signs as he passes, probably jump him or worse. Come here Hugh I say crawling to him. Listen, could I have a raincheck? I'm still a little queasy and it was a great moment and I could've gone with it but at this point a little sleep is sounding good. Do you mind Hugh? Oh Becky. Go ahead, sleep it off. He sounds sad. I take his hand. I use him as a pillow.

DAHLIA

I smell coffee. It makes me happy. But my stomach has a memory of its own. I don't get out of bed. I look out the window, gauge the daylight, think it's still morning, see a tall glass of water and some Advil on the nightstand, take a sip, down the caplets. Wonder what Hugh's doing. I get up. Go to the kitchen, to the coffeemaker in spite of my tummy. I am an addict.

Hugh's gone. He left a note. On the coffeemaker. Where I'd find it. He so knows me. Went to Dahlia's so you can work. Love, H. He's so thoughtful. He doesn't want to distract me.

I'm distracted. Embarrassed. Weirded out about last night. I think I'll go back to bed.

My boots are flung across my room. I must have done that. In my go mood. Before my personal stop sign made me step on the brakes. What is wrong with me? How could I let my chance with Hugh go like no big? I shouldn't worry about it. We're inevitable. I mean we've waited this long. I can't be worrying about it. I have to work.

I finish my coffee. I go to the bathroom. I look in the mirror. Pee. Look in the mirror again. My eyes are dim. You look like I feel. Max used to say that to me every morning when I stayed with him and Callie. I don't look that bad considering. I've lost track of my hair but the gold of it lights me up. I splash my face. Rub it hard with my towel. Hugh's towel, it's already wet, limp on the doorknob.

I slug some more coffee. I don't get dressed. I work just right. Naked painting myself naked. My Object of Desire. I swab acrylic indigo on canvas, it's just enough. I sever my hands from my arms and place the cut photo perfectly within the composition. I graft one of Max's beards onto my face. Dismembering and refusing pleases me. If I could do this in real life I could take my favorite pieces of everyone who means anything to me and make the perfect person. My hair. Hugh's eyes, his mouth, that part of his neck. Dahlia's hands. Her heart. Max's what? His wiriness, his transparency, his drama. No, Callie's drama.

She walked into a room and consumed it. Like the night I met Fred. Callie and I decided to go out to dinner. We planned to meet at Kelley & Ping, burn our mouths on some curry, drink some Thai beer to sting the heat away. I got there first and had some gunpowder tea at the bar which filled with smoke and wispy people waiting for tables. Callie was late and so was Fred's roommate and Fred and I started talking through the haze. I'm waiting for a nonsmoking table he said apologetically. Me too. He reminded me of Hugh a little but with brown eyes and a freer laugh. When Callie finally showed her long arms parted the frontdoor curtain and glowed into the dark bar, all eyes were on her et cetera. I have always had a certain effect on a room but I hate that kind of attention, don't know what to do with it, don't want it. Callie did. She was dragging her ruby coat and that train of hair behind her, aware that the bar crowd lowered its volume to let her in. When she came to sit next to me I worried Fred would defect. Callie wanted him to. Even when our table for 2 was ready she refused to leave Fred until his roommate came, buying time by asking me questions about Fred right in front of him, like he wasn't there, like he was privy to our girltalk about him, like there was a charge in the air. Which there was, and when Callie realized she wasn't part of it she patted her stomach and said Becky I'm totally starved, let's ask to be seated. Fred doesn't mind, he's a gentleman.

I didn't think twice about what she might have interrupted between Fred and me that first night. I could only see how Callie moved through life instantly knowing and getting what she wanted. And when she didn't she cut her losses, lavishly pretending she'd chosen the outcome. She was vivid at all times, like life could be infused with life, invented with whatever she had at her disposal, like boredom was not an option.

At Berkeley, whenever she was sick of studying, often, usually, she'd show up at my room at the coop, watch me work, closely watching, waiting for me to pause, to wonder what to do next with the fenders and hubcaps. I'd hammer them, twist them, rig them into shape, dangle neon tubes from the wreckage, green for go. What's this one called Becky? Red Light. Uh, Becky. Are you colorblind? She seemed sincere so I didn't snap at her. No Callie, I know it's green. She looked at it a little while longer. Why do you need the neon, it's garish, it looks better without it. I didn't tell her I wanted garish. I didn't tell her the piece was about the color. I didn't tell her it was our car that ran the light. I didn't exactly know that was why I was doing it. Until I got to New York, until I got to therapy, until I heard the words survivor guilt once a week for months. I said It needs color. I thought she understood color. She seemed to embody it. Everyone paled next to Callie. Her intensity. If I had met her without knowing her history I would've been surprised by her intensity. It didn't go with her Snow White face. Her adorable freckled nose. The first time I saw her touching it fanatically I thought she had a cold. But she kept doing it, no visible cold symptoms. Since I did know her history I just assumed she was a cokehead. I stopped giving it any thought. Until Dahlia, who'd just moved in with Callie at the time, clued me in. You know how she has that loftbed? I sleep on the floor, right under her. She's not loud or anything but she's not tactful either. She does it like every night. At first I noticed this rustling around up there and I thought she was just restless but then I'd notice how quiet it got. There's always this stillness in the room, both of us listening for her release. When I first caught on I thought she was rude, ok I thought she was sick, but then I realized it's how she puts herself to sleep. I don't mind, really. I feel sorry for her.

Dahlia's too generous. It bugs me that anything goes with her, she'll tolerate nightly masturbating and Max, even find a good reason for such extremes. It makes me feel like one of her causes when she buys my stuff. But only briefly. I know I make art that really means something to her. That makes me happy. I want Dahlia to be happy. She has that air of sexually abused people, that certainty, that power, that knowledge which she spares people from by being extremely vulnerable.

I've made one piece for my show that's just for her. I always do. It's my first and only performance selfportrait. It's called Lips Stick. I had her put on Paloma Red and leave her imprint all over me. Then I videotaped myself and took stills of the playback on TV. All that survived the cut and paste is my torso. The lip prints look like gouges in my body. The blue hue from the television screen casts the perfect ghoulish autopsy glow. It just turned out that way. Then I named it. Then I understood it was for Dahlia. It is Dahlia. She'll buy it. She'll put it in her bedroom. Her lovers, if and when, will think it's homoerotic. Dahlia will look at it when she wakes up from a bad dream about what her father did to her.

I showed it to her the second I finished it last week. She looked at it a long time and then she goes Yeah. We were standing side by side in front of it, I could see her in profile, very still, her eye getting wet. I reached up, put my arm around her neck, hauled her head down on my shoulder.

If only these last two were as clear to me. I study Object of Desire. The paint is all mood, indigo, swirling around behind my figure like I'm some Kahlo still life. Of all her work why did I liken myself to her cutopen fruit? That's just wacky, like I can't deal, like her self-portraits are too powerful a precedent to engage with, to reinterpret, to appropriate. Fuck it. I'm overanalyzing. I think it's done.

I should tackle my last piece now, I'm just not in the mood. I just don't have the energy. I'll do it later. I need a nap.

The phone is ringing somewhere far away. I'm moving through thick green air. I can't reach out. I so want to but I can't. I push myself until the force of the pushing makes my head tingle like I'm gonna cry. Or pee. The ringing stops. I hear my voice. Hi this is Becky and I'll be pissed if you don't leave a message. Hey Beck it's Dahlia scuffle And Hugh. We're going to Where are we going Dahlia? She laughs in the background. Yaffa! Hugh, I thought we rehearsed this Right, Yaffa. Come have lunch. You need to eat. They hang up before I can drag myself out of bed. Hmm, food, that doesn't sound half bad. Even some of that vegetarian slop Dahlia loves might hit the spot, like babyfood.

I walk down A. Fast, no eye contact, the bitchwalk Max taught me when I first came to New York. You know Becky New York is not California, it's not about who's the nicest. You can't walk around looking people in the eye and smiling at them. You probably even say Hi. He was right, but I didn't tell him that. Whatever selfpreservation instinct he was trying to instill in me happened. From dealing with him, not from following his instructions. But I learned. He took pride in how I turned out. He took credit.

I catch a glimpse of myself in the shop windows, see my speed, my determination, my core. My walk suits me. I am ambitious.

I think I'll swing by the gallery. See what Maya's doing to get ready for my show. See what the crowd's been like for the guy who preceded me. The sales. See what mood the artbuyers are in. Hugh and Dahlia can get along without me a little while longer.

I turn on 10th, see how the East Village is changing, see how the RENT tour probably saved, definitely ruined Life Cafe, see how the galleries that haven't gone bust or moved to the mall in Chelsea show decent work, hardcore challenging stuff not just what will sell like that. What's left in SoHo's totally Guggenheimized, beyond the reach of artists like me, the ones who aren't bankrolled, the ones who can't afford Pearl Paint anymore, the talents, the ones who can still draw, the grounded experimenters who will never turn our stuff into ovenmitts and umbrellas.

Standing in front of the gallery, a gleaming oasis propping up a stillscuzzy tenement, it's hard to imagine anyone with dough actually coming here. If you don't look too carefully it's great, my favorite kind of space, whitepainted brick walls, whitewashed woodslatted floors, lots of light streaming in, good visibility from the street to snag the walkins, the furs from Jersey who slum it on Saturday afternoons, while it's still light out, still safe.

Maya's in her office looking at somebody else's slides.

She peers up at me through one of them. Oh Becky, great. Sit down. Look at this. I take the slide from her and lean over the lighttable. I'm looking at watercolors of cats. You wouldn't believe the junk we get, unsolicited and otherwise. Yeah well you know Maya people think art's easy, and it is compared to being a waitress. She laughs and I see how yellow her teeth are, from drinking coffee all day. I use my tongue to measure the gunk on my own teeth. Maybe I'll cut down. A little. You have the right attitude about art Becky. Just make good stuff and don't take it too seriously. Of course that's not what the press release will say but leave that to me. She takes a long draw on a black coffee, offers me none, sets the cup down, her streaked blonde hair bobbing back into place. She looks me up and down, smiles with those teeth and says So?

So how was the turnout for Dannon's stuff? So so really. Painting is painting is painting you know? There just aren't that many interesting ways to abstract at this point. You have to be pretty utterly famous already to sell abstraction. She snaps off the lighttable, a giant cold diamond on her middle finger, her browned arms without an ounce of chub. Dannon's really good and he sold more than most of my artists but it's hard to be a painter and differentiate yourself. You of course don't have that problem. You have a unique product, if you'll excuse the expression. I'm calling your show The Naked and The Nude, per your suggestion. Great I say, I get to dis Kenneth Clark in public, the old man's archaic moralistic worldview, his false dichotomy, pure or salacious, high art or low. Maya puts her hand on mine. And Becky I'm toying with the idea of calling you neofigurative instead of a portraitist. She looks pleased with herself, her bluntended hair sharpening her arrogance, her pontificating. I mean Frida Kahlo was called a painter not a portraitist she says, touching her collarbone through her thin silk sweater, her voice a cigarette purr. Although the Cindy Sherman precedent in your work makes using the word portrait way less fey. Maya is smart, right about how I'm positioning myself post Cindy Sherman feminist didactic tirade. I'd like to reference the Starn twins, they're a great precedent and not just commercially. Oh please Maya, their images are so literal, such art history cliche. The only thing I like about them is the Scotch tape. Maya pauses. What about Witkin? she says, bracing. Well, his work is disturbing, and brilliant, but he's just so, so Catholic about the body ie guilty. Ok ok, I won't mention him either. But you will mention Hoch right? she's important to me. Becky is there anyone who isn't dead I can line you up with historically? preferably someone who sells? No one's doing what I'm doing Maya. Just say Cindy Sherman and collectors' ears will perk up. Yes yes. Maya's impatient, perpetually. She ejects from her chair, drops the cat slides into the trash.

Oh, listen, I've invited a couple of magazine writers but they always say they'll try and then don't show so don't get your hopes totally up. Um, Maya, aren't you supposed to be telling me how much you can do for me not how much you can't? You don't want bullshit Becky. This show will be very good for you, I told you that before. But I'm no Mary Boone, and you've gotta start somewhere. I mean you're what, almost 30? Not quite. But this is your first solo show, so you're no prodigy. But you've got vision, and you make a pretty package. I'll get you enough publicity. You will take off.

That's all I want. I choose to ignore her packaging concept, how she will commodify me. As insane as I am getting ready Maya, I'm totally into it, and it sure beats 9 to 5. Yeah, well, who wouldn't give up their day job Becky but yours actually has you well positioned for Europe. All those little galleries that deposit their artists' slides in your bank, after I launch you here, you've got entree into Paris, Milan, London, maybe Prague if the money stays good there. I imagine myself hauling around a giant diamond on my finger. It looks good. Solos abroad then you come back here in a year or so and a serious gallery'll pick you up. I hang my imaginary futurework in the little MoMA space, where pets go. I imagine Hilton Kramer's review, Artforum's, imagine my old teachers seeing me hung there, imagine how the Collage Pet will react, how my friends will. How Callie will. She'll read about me in The Observer, go irresistibly to my work, realize how fabulous it is, I am. She'll regret Fred, she'll regret how she tried to turn me into a major character in her minor little drama of a life, how I turned myself into an excharacter, claimed my own life on a bigger stage. I can't wait. Maybe I shouldn't, this show's big enough for a magazine writer it should be big enough for Callie.

Maya's saying I'll broker that for you, that's what I'm here for Becky. Just don't fuck me over because I can help you but I can also hurt you. Geez Maya, relax. Let me get through this before you start with the threats and vendetta. Listen Becky, you're not gonna remember half of what I've said to you when you open, you're in a radically altered state right now and it'll be like that until you close. So all you have to remember is this one thing, keep me on your side. Maya, I'm completely in your hands. She beams at me. Well, Maya, thanks for the friendly pep talk but I gotta go now, I'm late for some people. Art people? No, friends. Oh. I get up to make my escape. Hey Maya, think it's too late to get an invitation sent to somebody who wasn't on the original list? Should I messenger it? are they in the business? No, another friend. Oh. Her disappointment with my puny artworld status makes me worry no one will come, gives me a little twinge of What if people hate my work? What if they laugh at it, at me? What if Callie sees me humiliated, rejected, a victim of my own vain desire to gloat? Like that's gonna happen. Maya won't let me bomb. Man I'm a wreck. Yeah sure Becky, I'll pop it in the mail, no sweat, but no guarantee it'll get there in time for the opening. I know, if it does it does.

Yaffa is a visual assault. Fakecloud ceilings, zebraskin booths, lamps that drip oil around a coy, stacked Venus. If I don't throw up now I'm not gonna. I do like the tabletops, laminated pen and ink nudes, they pose arrogantly in a garden of hair and roses.

Hugh and Dahlia are sitting with their heads too close together. I stop short of their table and just stand there, see how long it takes them to notice me. It takes too long. They're laughing about something and stop when

I clear my throat. Dahlia goes It lives. Dahlia I wasn't really drunk I was nervous ok? so give me a break already, I'm in a radically altered state right now. I try to give Hugh a special look. He stands up and pulls a chair from another table going Poor baby, sit down and get some food in you, you'll feel better. That's better I say like I deserve to be pampered. What's good here Dahl? Dahlia's eyes look up and circle around as she recites the menu. Dahlia's not vegetablecentric because it's cheap or she's nostalgic for Berkeley. Dahlia never went to Berkeley, she never went to college. She was dancing. In New York. She was obsessing over her body, perfecting it, cleansing it, her health, distracting herself from everything with motion. Hugh leans way back in his chair, plugging his nose every time Dahlia names something, or fakegagging or pointing at the back of his throat. Hmm. I'll just have coffee. I notice the tea strainers on their saucers. They do have coffee here don't they? We wouldn't do that to you Becky. Get a hummus too. That'll go down. And stay down Hugh chides. Yum, mashed chickpeas. What the hell. I can't think of anything I really want to eat.

The coffee and mush and pita come right away and I'm glad. The last thing I want is to have nothing to do while I sit here wondering if Hugh told Dahlia about last night. I hope not. I want to tell her. I could bring it up. I'm among friends. No, that would be indelicate. Hugh's in a good mood and I don't want to make him more selfconscious than he already is. Although I do want to tell them what I did about Callie. I'll choose my moment, spring it on them, awe them with my aplomb, win their gratitude, at least Dahlia's. I'll eat first, have my coffee.

The waitress forgot my half and half. I see her out in the backyard under a 20s cabaret fresco, smoking like she has to. I wave at her like some deranged relative at the airport. She doesn't see me. Or ignores me. I decide to get it myself. I go to the sordid little counter. The cash register's covered in leopard and a brass plaque that says Please ask for your free Yaffa condom. Shit. If only we'd come here yesterday. I look over my shoulder to get Hugh's attention, he has to see this. Dahlia's saying something in his ear. Which really bugs me. I mean fine, they're friends, but I don't do that kind of stuff, tell secrets in front of people. Dahlia doesn't usually play those games either. And I know she's not into Hugh. I mean they had their chance in high school and nothing came of it, why would it now? But it still pisses me off. I want them to know I know something's up. I'm not blind.

I spot a little creamer pot on a table near ours and

sashay back to them, plop what looks disappointingly like skim milk into my cup. So, what's going on you guys? Hugh looks at Dahlia all meaningful. Dahlia looks at me and goes You seem pretty nervous Becky, you ok? Yeah, I'm decent all things considered. Good because Hugh and I have been thinking Hugh and you? Her face doesn't change guiltily or anything. Yeah, we'd like to make a little preopening soiree for you at my place, to take your mind off, well, you know. Just let me know who you'd like to have around you, who can help you get through the waiting around for your opening. Like there's anyone else who could. Now I feel like a total bitch, they've been plotting nothing more behind my back than how to make me less of a basketcase. I throw my arms around their necks, hug them hard. I love you guys. We love you too I get back in stereo.

I sit back in my chair, happy as a clam, in spite of my thin discolored coffee. Hugh goes Becky you're not gonna ask the pitbull to come are you? I mean after last night don't you think you're not exactly obligated? I think about Max for a microsecond before skipping to the real event of last night, wondering if Hugh's thinking about it too. I slide my boot toward him under the table, tap him with my suede toe. He smiles all shy. I go Max is not likely to make me less of a basketcase so it's not an issue Hugh. His eyes move from me to Dahlia, he takes a sip of tea and goes Good, I'm not exactly thrilled by the prospect of being in the same room with the man again. Poor Hugh I coo, forget about him. He's a major loser sometimes. No offense Dahl. She shrugs.

She had the bad judgment to actually sleep with Max. They had this torrid thing that totally threw Callie. Callie and Max had been broken up about 6 months. Dahlia was at the start of her slumming phase, living with Callie, and knew all about Max from Callie's crying jags and 3am rages which had finally petered out. Dahlia and Max had never met until my first little group show at PS1 which I should never have invited Max to but Callie insisted. She said she was over him, she could handle it, it would be good for her, I should help her any way I could. But Dahlia and Max have always had this weird rapport and it started that night. Dahlia recognized Max from all the shredded pictures. Max was eating the free pretzels and Dahlia walked right over to him and accidentally spilled her wine on his leather pants. Callie was thrilled but not as much as Max who really got off on it when he got what was going on. He started calling Dahlia, hanging up whenever Callie answered.

Dahlia started seeing Max. Of course Callie found

out about it. Not from me. She saw them together at Fez and they had a big scene. It was sick and everybody knew it. Except Hugh who only got Callie updates secondhand from me and I left out the unflattering details to spare Dahlia. Dahlia finally broke it off with Max not because of Callie but because Max was always trying to tell her what to do and Dahlia stopped liking that.

Dahlia shrugs. It was what it was she says. Now it's something else. She and Max got beyond it, they're friends. Dahlia has a knack for keeping and getting rid of the right people in her life. Mostly.

I put down my cup, I go all dramatic, I go So I did it you guys. I invited Callie. Dahlia's cheeks bloom, she's smiling like the superior being she is. I've done the right thing. For me. For all of us. Well Hugh's less effusive, for him it's not so huge. Callie's been out of his backyard for years, half a decade, longer than anyone was even close to Callie. He rubs the back of my neck and goes So you're gonna get it over with huh? I guess that's what this is Hugh. If not we're all in trouble.

Becky. Yeah. Max? Yeah. Listen, sorry about last night ok? are you still mad? I don't know what I am Max. A little hyper over my show mainly. I plop down in my boudoirchair. Max's voice revives my exhaustion, last night's exhaustion et cetera. I know Becky, I'm sure it's insanity getting ready, I wasn't thinking about that last night, I was thinking about Dahlia. I've been a little worried about her around this Callie thing. I really think it has something to do with her father, like she needs to see some justice done in some relationship in her life, and she can do it in this sort of innocuous way with Callie in a way she can't with her father. This actually makes sense, when did Max get so wise. Not that I'm about to let him know I think so. You might be right Max, but why can't she just do a one woman show about it like everyone else? or stop taking her father's money? And why couldn't you have said all this last night, I might not have reacted so badly. I know Becky, I should've, that's why it's called an apology. Ok Max, I'm fine with it, really, I know you did it for Dahlia. In fact I'm so fine with it I went to the gallery today, they're sending the invitation. Oh yeah? you really did that? Yeah. Wow. There's a long pause. I try to sound relaxed. So what's up with you Max? The usual. Trying to get auditions and stuff. This morning's cattlecall went nowhere he says all dismayed. I'm thinking last night's tequila might have had something to do with it but I don't say that. I wrap the phonecord around my pinkie. You still need new head-shots? Well yeah. You offering? Yeah, why not. After my show. You're on. So you spending the whole day working or you wanna get some coffee? I taste my teeth. You know what, I just got back from coffee. Oh. Is Hugh there? You wanna have coffee with Hugh? Right. What I was getting at is are you alone. Oh, yeah, Hugh's out with Dahlia getting some stuff for a little thing at Dahlia's tomorrow night. You coming? You want me there? Oh Max, don't be absurd, I love you even when I hate you. Me too Becky. Well so maybe I could stop by, like before he gets home? I have something for you. What? You'll see. A present? Yeah, so stop asking me about it. If you're bearing gifts, you can come any time. Anyway, Hugh's going to the Joyce with Dahlia tonight so he won't be back till late. Hugh likes dance? I have no idea. He's just trying to stay out of my hair. Then he's an idiot. Max don't be petty. But it's so much fun. Max. Ok, so I'll stop by later. Ok but maybe we really should make it a lot later, I do have to finish today. Sure. What time's good Becky, you name it.

I don't know what to call it. I don't know what it is. My last piece is giving me the most trouble. I don't know what to do. I can't put it off anymore. I'm running out of time.

I taped a rectangle of raw canvas to my wall. I pasted my fulllength body left of center. My hair streams down me Rapunzellike, Botticellilike. I am golden. This is wrong. It's overtly beautiful, distressing. This is not what I wanted it to be.

I start covering it with Vermillion, Viridian. I stop.

I stare at it. I'm too anxious. I can't see beneath the surface of it. I have to keep looking. I can't. If I could I'd bolt from the room, from my apartment, my skin. How can I resolve a problem I can't define? Something's missing, or too much. The composition's good, the hues are glorious, rich, textured. I move in close, examine the canvas inch by inch. Try to lose perspective. I do.

I'm lost. I don't know what the fuck this is, what it means to me, how the image even popped into my head in the first place. This so pisses me off that I could really harm it, take a knife to it, a brush, do a de Kooning and paint out the beauty, leave a horrible cartoon there. I could.

I can't. I can't wreck it. Maya wants 6 pieces and this is the biggest, it's too late to start over, print more autonudes, try something else. What I have to try is another way of seeing this. Maybe if I see it in context, with the others, as a piece of a larger whole, my socalled vision. I do a Matthew Arnold, remove myself from a vacuum. I surround the problem collage with the finished ones, arrange them on my walls, surround myself with me. I stand there turning, looking, still not seeing. I don't go near my brushes. Fear spreads from my stomach to my fingertips. I'm practically vibrating. My head feels liquid. I can't take it. I panic. I call Dahlia. Hi, it's Dahlia, leave a message. I hang up. I call Max. Hi it's me. Becky? Yeah. What's wrong, you sound a tad I am Max, feel like coming by now? You're not using me as a distraction are you. You bet. I need one big time. Ok, sure. And Max, don't say anything when you come in, just come sit with me for a little while? Sure his voice massages. I'll be right there.

I avoid looking at my pieces. This is not easy. It is. I open my window, lean on the fire escape like an old lady, breathe, look for Max's shape at the corner of 13th and A, will him onto my street. He doesn't show of course, it's too soon. I watch the dealers hog the phone booths, wonder how their pants stay up, wonder if the one rolledup pantleg is some gangsta signal, hear a siren go by, watch the dealers' backs curl into the receivers, see their lack of fear, their cold assessment of how much they can get away with, envy them, their cool clarity, their sense of purpose, their knowledge of the game, their impunity, how little they wouldn't do to get what they want. I will learn their ways, their look, I'll get a tele-photo, capture them, seize them, make them mine, do a show of them abroad where they won't see that I've taken their pictures, so they won't think I've betrayed them, so they won't think I'll give my negs to the cops, so I won't be in danger of some kind of The buzzer scares the shit out of me. I say Max to the intercom. He says Tis I. I push the button, release the door downstairs, let him in. He'll climb the 5 flights, he's claustrophobic. He'll spurn the elevator. He'll get here fast, he doesn't smoke anymore, his legs are strong. I remember them straddling the junk heap. I remember the pictures. His legs look sturdy, lean, like I like'em. I can't keep my mind from looking at the center of the frame, the obvi-ous, what dominates the image in my memory. I have thought of it before, have had its talents suggested to me by 2 different women, have never felt aroused by the prospect of it. I do now. What is wrong with me? I have to snap out of this before he walks through my door. I'm losing it.

I hear a quiet tapping. I compose myself. I open the door. He kisses me on the cheek. I smell his wet hair, feel his hands holding my arms while he pecks me innocently on my other cheek which is slightly burning. Max. Thanks for coming.

His eyes get big as he walks into my livingroom, sees all my collages taped to the walls. You're the first one to see them all Max. He takes in a breath like he's gonna say something, I put my finger to my lips to shush him. I see him look at my body, at the paint, the shadows, the cuts and pastes. He doesn't say a word, honors my request, me. His face tells me what I need to know. He loves my pieces. They're good.

When can I talk? At the opening. They're fair game then. He walks over to where I'm gripping the back of my diningchair. He taps my knuckles with his finger like a wand, makes me release, grips my arm, steers me to my couch. We sit down, he puts his arm around me, keeps looking at the walls. He's waiting for me to say something, to change the subject, or not. I don't. Not yet. I like his arm there, I like my collages, like my couch, my diningchairs and table, the undershirt I put on, the way my hair feels on my back, how I'm pinned a little by Max's arm.

Have a drink with me Max. Hair of the dog or celebration? Consummation. Of what? Our friendship. He squeezes me to his side and leans his head on mine. I go How about an Amaretto on ice? Yum. Got any cherries? Nope, is that how you like it? Oh yes. I'll walk over to A and hunt some up. Forget it Max, don't bother. He lifts his arm off me, stands up. Actually Becky, whatcha doing for dinner? I could cook up something, something basic. I'd love that Max, but I have to keep working, I'm not quite finished. Really? He looks around again, dazzled I can see. This spurs me on. I won't be much longer now I think. He looks at me like Your call. What're you cooking Max? Big fat steak? Mmmmm, that would be perfect. Baked potatoes and garlicbread with that? Why not. Red wine? You got it. And do not even think of trying to give me money Becky. This is on me. I'd like to be on you Max. He smiles at me all boyish, a dissonant look on Max. Then he leaves, leaves the door ajar, makes a quick noise in the corridor, pops his head back into my hallway. Don't you want your present? You kidding? He pushes the door open. He hands me a plank of Earth. Thought you might like to do some entertaining when you're a famous artist. It takes me a minute, then I see what it is. I take it to my table, push the paint tubes aside, wedge a spackling knife into the slit in the center of the world, start prying. Max goes Whoa hold it, there's a lever underneath. He gently opens my table and puts the leaf inside.

It was in storage, Callie never knew I had it. Now you can seat 8! You're a doll Max. You are Becky. He touches my arm. I'll be back in a few.

I go back to my brushes. I spot the Mars Black among the tubes of Indigo, Iridescent Gold, Viridian, Acra Red. I pick up the tube, take it to the obstinate collage which looks good next to the fire escape. I screw the cap off the black, squeeze the color out a bit, dab it right on my head. I'm anxious again but good anxious, alert, humming. I smear the pigment, with my fingers, fast, stroke the golden head until it's gone, streak it with noncolor, shade, shadow. My skin pales by contrast. This is good. But my arms dangle naturally, exquisitely. I get my matteknife, slice them off, get my Elmer's, glue them back on the wrong sides of my body. My hands overlap my pelvis. I get that feeling, that weird chill. I step back. I look at it from the couch. I look at it from the corner. From the hallway. I go back to it. See that I dribbled a little paint on my face. Wait for it to dry so I can scrape it off.

I go out onto my fire escape. Look in my window. See a new composition. Like Botticelli's Venus my figure is rising. But this is AntiVenus. This is good. This is Monumental Vanity, to appropriate Hoch's wrongly titled series. I've made the image that lives up to her idea. This is what I wanted. But it still lacks depth. I can't see into it. I climb back in, take a fat wide brush, gob shimmery gold onto the bristles, shake it like a wand at the canvas, back up, hold my breath, wait, wait, don't panic, don't look away, keep looking, pounce on the canvas, take my matteknife to it, scrape off the paint spatters and smears, scare myself with the blade, stop the scraping, before it's too late, before I puncture the surface, I catch myself, catch my breath. I pick up my brush, still wet and lustrous. I edge the canvas with iridescence. I rest.

Before I can overthink it I call my smallfry dealer who thinks she can change my life. They're ready Maya. Marvelous Becky. I'll send someone for them, don't leave. I don't tell her the paint's not even dry. It will be. Maya's excited, she's been waiting for this moment, she says He'll have to crate them so they don't get creased so make sure he doesn't screw up the edges when they go in. Your edges are important. She's right, she gets my stuff. Too bad she's so cutthroat. Maybe. Don't you want to see them before he picks them up? No. It'll only make you nervous to have me walk into your little apartment and scrutinize them. Let me do that at the gallery, alone. I'll let you know if there are any minor adjustments to be made. They are good, aren't they

Becky, I expect them to be good. They're good Maya. That's what I like to hear from my artists.

So, I'm ready. For anything. Everything.

Max comes back with his arms full of groceries. He almost drops them when he sees my bare walls. The craters are working carefully but fast, each collage occupying its own sector of the floor until they box it. Max runs his eyes over them again. Wow, when you decide something that's it, no second thoughts. This is like a stab and I panic, shout Hold it! at the craters. All my euphoria is instantly over. Is that your not so veiled opinion that I should have second thoughts? No no no Becky, not at all. I'm impressed by your confidence, that's all. I like how he sees me, I'm relieved. He sets the bags down on the table and reaches out his hand walking backwards into the kitchen like I'm to follow him. I wave my hands at the craters to erase my last command. Max starts rifling my drawers saying I better open this wine and fast or you're gonna stroke out. You're just like me before a performance. You need to be totally indulged tonight. I wonder what he has in mind exactly. I remind myself this is Max. He pours me some Cab and says Just take a glass of this and turn on some music and lie down on that girlie couch of yours. I do as he says, listening to him rattling my pans, listening to the craters finishing up, listening to Benny Goodman's clarinet loop up and down some scales.

I'm drifting, letting pictures flash inside my closed eyes, my collages, my friends, Max's face which is constantly changing. When I open my eyes he's leaning against my kitchen wall, a glass of beautifully crimson wine in his hand, smiling. I smile. That's more like it he says. Oh Max, why have we taken so long to do this, to call a truce? Yeah, and what were we fighting about anyway? I have no idea at the moment, and I don't want to remember I say. He walks toward me, leans down, touches his glass to mine. To forgetting the past he says. To putting it behind us and leaving it there I say.

I lean toward the mirror, taste last night's garlicbread, taste Max's secret steak marinade through today's several coffees, brush my teeth for the 3rd time today, hope Max stumbled home ok after drinking most of the wine he brought over. I watch my hand tremble, run the liquid liner across my lid, feel the cool wetness, keep my eye halfclosed, do the other, lean against the open bathroom door, wait till I'm dry. There's something holy in anticipation. I am all potential, all possibility, all verge and brink. I feel powerful, incredibly humble, unbelievably scared.

I'm nervous, sad, like I've lost something. I want to cry. In my mother's arms. Crawl into her lap, feel her fingers comb my hair, hear her tell me not to worry, everything will turn out fine. I was 7 when my parents screeched into oblivion, a child, only potential. I know them from pictures. I memorized their faces, see them in mine in the mirror, see a black teardrop fall to the floor, disappear on the dirty tile.

And then it's over. Like all my connections to the past. Fleeting, gone. That's ok. Memory hurts.

I wash my face with icewater. Start over. Eyeliner, blush, earrings, naked, wondering what to put on now. Hugh was wearing khakis and a new green sweater when he left to help Dahlia cook. Not that I can go by Hugh, he doesn't know from clothes. I want to be festive, be feted, be careless, unbreakable. I look in my closet, look for something to clothe my mood, consider my coat and nothing else, what the hell, my body won't exactly be private after tomorrow. I haven't heard from Maya. I hope that's a good thing. It must be.

I try the handmedown Missoni pants I got from Dahlia, I kick them off, slide on my blue satin slipdress, shimmer around the apartment, decide it doesn't go with my badgirl eyeliner, shrug it off, toss it on my bed. I tie on my red velvet halterdress, feel like a flame, feel my hair tickle my back, feel like laughing, feel around in my closet, get my strappy shoes, my little purse. Throw my coat over my bare shoulders. Grab my keys. Look around my apartment before closing my door.

I am savoring this, myself as I am, before my big moment, before exposure. I am on the verge of my life, of becoming something new. I hold on to the feeling like wine on my tongue, like the wine I will sip with my friends who are waiting for me. I savor my neighbors sitting out on their stoops, savor the blocks between me and Dahlia, the dusklight on her building, the sounds of people in the park, yelling, swinging on creaking chain, drumming an African heartbeat. They're so alive, and I am, and we're related by that, by virtue of breathing.

I step into Dahlia's building knowing the people who love me are here, waiting for me, expectant. I picture their faces when they see me, glad, smiling, I imagine their arms around me, holding me as I hold them now, dear, close. I buzz Dahlia, hear her canned voice say Beck? I feel my heart full, my throat, manage Yeah. The inner door clicks, I push on it, wanted. I push for the elevator, picture Max as he climbed the stairs, picture Hugh and Dahlia as they hauled up groceries and wine, laughing over the hum and clack of the elevator to the highest floor that's all Dahlia's, talking about how to make my party nice, for me. I go to Dahlia's door, find it open, slightly, push it gently, hear the sound of my sweet friends' voices, it builds as I enter, hang my coat on the iron hook, follow their warm murmur to the kitchen. I stand at the threshold, lean on a frenchdoor watching them all busy. Max turns, sees me. Becky! They all turn. They rush to me, hold me.

Dahlia pushes my hair away from my ear, whispers Liz and Stuart are here, out in the diningroom, I hope it's ok, she called and Hugh answered and she was dying to meet him and I didn't feel I could lie about why we were busy tonight so I asked them. Do you mind? As much as I like Dahlia whispering in my ear I wish she was telling me a good secret, something I wanted to hear. Liz and Stuart are fine, but they don't go with my dress, my mood, my neediness. I look at Dahlia's open face, push her hair back from her ear, whisper Don't worry about it, hope my face doesn't show my deflation.

At least there's wine. The soiree being at Dahlia's means icky Dahlia food that Hugh didn't talk her out of. Artichoke dip and wholewheat pita. Eggplant strips,

5grain bread. Dahlia's rubbing her hands together and saying I have a barley and bulgur casserole in the oven!

We order takeout. From 3 different restaurants because of all the food allergies and aversions. Max and Hugh actually agree to share an entree. This is the least of what they've shared, but this time it's consensual. Dahlia pops a cork, yells Quick get a flute! Hugh rushes at her with a stem, nuzzles the neck of the bottle with it. Dom streams into the glass, fizzes lightly. Dahlia hands it to me. I imagine bathing in it, feeling the pop of its bubbles on my skin, in my eyes and mouth, opening both, drinking it in and seeing through it, everything golden, bright. Max carries 5 more glasses at once, his waiterself showing. Liz turns down the bubbly, the rest of us stand around the kitchen sipping. Unappealing food smells emanate from Dahlia's Magic Chef. She opens the ovendoor, removes the offending casserole, says I'll freeze this for later. She floridly opens her wrapdrawer, pulls out a huge box of plastic, pulls out way more than she needs, lets its transparent length dangle there. Hugh blushes, does not look at me. Dahlia tilts her head toward her drawer, goes I'm very well stocked. I told Dahlia this afternoon what happened with Hugh. Now he knows she knows. I hope he's not mad. She's not ribbing him, us. The joke's on herself, she's been sexually moot for ages.

Wrapped roses pile high on the counter. For me. From my wonderful, indulgent, thoughtless friends. I'm looking around the sink for rubber gloves. I can't risk a prick and no one's helping. Max doesn't know about my bloodphobia, at least not from me, but you'd think it would dawn on Dahlia that I can't do the roses myself. Or Hugh. I clear my throat at Dahlia. Got any gloves? You don't have to wash the Oh Beck, I'm sorry, I wasn't thinking. She collects the bundles, takes them to the sink, unwraps the gorgeous buds, releasing their fragrance. I close my eyes, to savor one sense at a time, to avoid seeing Dahlia prick herself. I wait, listening for the sound of water filling a vase. I don't hear it. I can't risk looking. I wait some more. I hear scissors snipping stems, Dahlia's being thorough. I feel something piercing the mass of my hair. I open my eyes, see my friends, huddled around me, each with a handful of smooth shortstems. They decorate my hair, up and down the length of it. They decorate me. I feel the weight of the stems tugging at my scalp, feel jittery and can't help but say You sure you got all the thorns Dahl? Don't worry Becky, I know how to take care of you. I open my eyes.

Just when you think Becky can't get any more beautiful Max trails off. Hugh shoots him a possessive look. I hope I can live up to the flowers. I hope I'm beaming, I must be, I feel shining, alight. I love you guys I say. Don't get all sentimental yet Dahlia commands, I think the food's here and I don't want to miss a Becky meltdown. She glides to her intercom.

Finally all the delivery boys have come and gone and we spread out on Dahlia's heavy oak dining table. She can seat 12. Tonight we are 6 and hungry. I decide Liz and Stuart make a good buffer, in case Max and Hugh relapse. We scoop food from cartons, dozens of them gape open around the table. Dahlia has a whole room just for a table and chairs. She has rustic crockery from Provence. She has ivory chopsticks, heavy burntmetal flatware, heavy thick wineglasses which we clink together. To a wildly successful show Becky. Hugh goes May it bring you an avalanche of praise. Max goes May it make you filthy rich and famous. Dahlia blows me a kiss and says May it bring you happiness. I go May it take care of that little matter we've all been so preoccupied with.

What little matter? Liz wants to know. She and Stuart have no idea what we're talking about but they deserve to be warned. I look around the table but no one volunteers. I brought it up, I guess it's my job. I go Callie may be at the opening you guys. Liz's face constricts, sterns. No way. Sorry to say way. It's just a question of whether she gets the invitation. Hugh adds And whether she'll come. Right. Max goes That's a big if. Why did you do that? Liz is freaked. She will never appreciate the simple beauty of our plan so I have no intention of telling her about it. Callie was on an old mailing list I inadvertently gave the gallery. Hugh looks at me like he can't believe I can lie. I make a dufus face at him like What else can I do? No one contradicts me. Liz goes Well I'm really glad you told me because I just couldn't go knowing she might be there. Liz. No, really. That would just be too painful and as much as I want to support you Becky, I can't do that to myself, we just can't do it. Stuart looks like he'll be starting an argument with her as soon as they get home. But Liz always wins. Gee, I'm sorry you both feel that way I say looking at Stuart. His arms are straight out in front of him, palms together. He opens them, hingepinkied, helpless, his wedding ring thick, obvious. I understand I say, think how rigid Liz is, how she's intractable enough to miss my opening over this, how inviting Callie has already made me choose her over two of my minor but current friends.

This freaks me out a little since that's what Callie used to do to me on purpose, pit my allegiance to her against everything else. Everyone. When Dahlia had the fling with Max, Callie kicked her out but that wasn't enough to make Callie less miserable. Or me. Callie was in a constant rage over it and spent every moment we were together going over and over what had happened. She even went to therapy finally, which was good, she got to obsess about it with someone besides me. Callie had some idea she might be responsible for Max and Dahlia's fascination with each other, but she just puked it out for months without really understanding a thing. I thought Dahlia was an idiot, mainly because I couldn't see what she saw in Max, but it was also a rotten thing to do to Callie. Dahlia knew it too but she couldn't help herself for some reason and I got to hear all about it constantly from her too. At first Callie insisted I stop being friends with Dahlia. She gave me an ultimatum. We were at her place painting her brick wall black and she goes You know Becky, if you really cared about me you'd stop seeing Dahlia. I mean how can you like her after what she's done to me? She had a point but they were all so into it I figured deep down they really wanted this to be happening so I played my part and let everyone cry on my shoulder. Except Max. Eventually Callie realized she could use me to her advantage. She'd ask me about Max and Dahlia. I'd tell her there was nothing to tell, that I didn't want to know about it from Dahlia, but Callie didn't buy that Dahlia wouldn't confide in me anyway which of course she did. So Callie tried a different tack and made me promise to tell Dahlia stuff that wasn't true like how Callie was bingeing and purging over it or smoking crack or suicidal. I promised her but I never did it. I just told Dahlia the same basic stuff about Callie that she already knew and vice versa and then I got sick of them both so I stopped returning their calls. One day Dahlia left me a reasonably abject message that she'd finally broken up with Max, which made me like her again, and since I wasn't being used in Callie's warped little game anymore I made up with her too. Then I got them back together. They were a little careful with each other at first but then that faded and they were back doing the latenight thing all over town and really close, maybe even doing a little Maxbashing but I didn't ask. I was just happy everything was back to normal.

I just want everyone to get along. Like tonight. We're getting along, we're divvying up the takeout, giving each other nibbles from our chopsticks, drinking lots of good wine. It's weird how we're all here at the table enjoying the meal but the person who made us all matter to each other is missing. Like somebody whited Christ out of the Last Supper.

My food is yummy, spicy, as hot as I can stand it. Max and I are the only ones eating Thai. I'm tempted to gargle my wine but don't, make the gargle gesture at Max, see if he'll do it. He doesn't, he brings me water. Thanks Max, I didn't even know I wanted that. That's what we're here for Beck.

What's your new work like? Stuart wants to know. I'm still doing collages, nudes that reference other nudes but from the subject's point of view. Stuart looks lost and I'm thinking maybe he's not sorry they're missing my opening. I think maybe I'll check my machine to see if Maya's called. Stuart goes Do you have to be an art historian to get them? Max goes Nope, grinning. I'd rather not talk about it anymore you guys. Stuart leans over and hugs me awkwardly. Sorry Becky. You must be nervous. Yeah I say, looking for Dahlia's cordless. So let's eat and drink and forget about tomorrow Max commands. He lifts the wine bottle and tilts it toward Hugh who puts his hand on top of his glass. Why can't he just say No thanks? I wonder if Max is thinking this too.

Dahlia's talking to Stuart about the bar exam for some reason. I get up to find the phone, speeddial myself, find no messages, what a relief, head back to the table, see Liz slyly checking out Hugh who catches her looking and doesn't have the sense not to ask So how did you meet Callie? Everyone stops talking. Liz looks nervously around the table like she's about to violate an oath or something. The rest of us know the whole story but we wait to hear what she'll say, if she'll say. We used to work together she offers, trying to give Hugh a pat answer. Oh really, where was that? Hugh's knowledge of Callie's life post him has too many gaps and he's genuinely curious about her all of a sudden. Or maybe he's arming himself for tomorrow night. No, not Hugh. Liz hesitates. Callie was the office manager at the mortgage company where I was then. She wasn't very organized and got fired almost right away. I felt sorry for her and lent her some money which I never do. She'd call from time to time. She was very funny, I really liked chatting with her. Liz looks at her plate, like having liked Callie is embarrassing. Stuart puts his arm around her. She looks at him, then back at Hugh. I'm thinking she's about to launch. I show my empty glass to Dahlia who

pours and pours. I lean back in my hardwood chair, trying to sip and kick Hugh without spilling. He's all
earnestly waiting for Liz to plod on, his elbow on the
table, shins out of reach.

Liz goes The day finally came that she could pay me
back and we decided to get together socially. She was
dating this lawyer who was fairly conservative, nice guy.
Stuart and I went out with them a few times. Callie
knew how to have a good time, and she could always
draw Stuart out of his shell, he's on the shy side. She pats
Stuart's hand. It balls up. Liz takes a baby sip of wine, to
minimize downtime, goes The first time I remember
thinking anything was off about Callie was this one time,
the 4 of us went to the Vanguard. We were having such
a good time until it became obvious that Callie and the
drummer couldn't take their eyes off each other and the
lawyer, Jim, wasn't it Honey? Stuart nods. Well, Jim
stormed out. I started to send Stuart after him and Callie
goes Liz don't be simpleminded, how do you think a guy
like that stays interested in someone like me. Stuart and
I couldn't believe how calculating she was, could we
Honey. Stuart shakes his head. That was in like January.

I look at all the heads turned toward Liz, engaged.
Callie's taking over my party and she's not even here. I
know it's my fault for bringing her up but this is ridicu-

lous. What's wrong with these people? Can't they see Callie's a tangent we don't want to get off on? Hugh's out of toe range. I raise my eyebrows at Max, at Dahlia, but they don't look at me, they're rapt, they're into Liz, into Callie. I'm downing my wine, counting the months left to go till the inevitable, wondering if Liz plans to relive them in something close to real time. I detour with What's for dessert Dahl? Frozen yogurt Beck. Dahlia snaps out of it, blinks, looks at everyone's plates. Is everybody done with dinner? Hugh goes No, actually, I'm still eating. He picks up a sparerib, it hovers over his plate which is covered with food from all over the world. Holding the rib's an empty gesture, he doesn't want food. He turns to Liz. What happened to the lawyer?

Liz looks redeemed, says Well, her eyebrows arched and ardent, on Valentine's Day Stuart and I were having a quiet candlelit dinner at home when the phone rang. I slide down in my chair, try one last desperate time to reach Hugh, nudge him to change the subject, appalled that Liz won't stop, can't. Liz is saying We let the machine pick up but it was Callie, crying and saying it was over with Jim and she just couldn't be alone. So we picked up and said Of course, come right over. When she got there and saw the remains of our little romantic dinner she started crying all over again and saying Oh why can't I ever last with anyone? Stuart suggested we all go out to take her mind off her troubles, he's such a sweetheart, so we went to this nice bar in our neighborhood and Callie drank too much mostly and we got stuck with the bill. Anyway, here we're thinking Jim finally got sick of her rollercoaster ride but it's Callie who ended it. And from then on, on Valentine's Day, we'd always end up with her one way or another. It was our fault for not just saying no to her but she always seemed to be in such a crisis, we didn't feel we could let her be alone, as if she had nowhere else to go. We didn't know about all of you at the time.

Heads are bobbing around the table. Mine too, that's just how Callie was, crisisprone, and you were the only one she could turn to. A rose falls from my head. I bend to get it. 3 more fall. This cracks me up. No one seems to notice me dangling. I look at everyone's shoes, think how like their inhabitants they are, loosen the straps on mine, slip them off.

I hear Hugh go So how did she finally alienate you Liz? I sit up for this. Too fast. Liz's face is completely animated now, it's lost its zombie rigor mortis. She looks like I feel, a little drunk, but she's barely even drinking. Callie started coming over a lot, staying really late, wanting to sleep over and stuff. When she'd been with Jim she was a real yuppie but every time she started seeing someone new she'd start to turn into him, take on his interests and his look. Hugh's head's still bobbing. I try to remember if Callie was dressed like him in his shrine to her at the coop. Sweaters, jeans, she was, but then we all dressed like that at Berkeley. If only Liz's voice had lost its zombie drone. I didn't think anything of her chameleon makeovers till she wasn't seeing anyone and started doing it with me. Stuart's nodding now. It was great at first, she always wanted to do whatever I wanted to do. She was my closest friend she says wistfully, without irony. Liz has no irony. But then she kept wanting to borrow my clothes, it's not like we're even the same size or anything. Liz has always been a gloater about her petiteness, her selfdenial.

She leans toward Hugh, her voice higher, tighter. One morning, Callie'd spent the night, I came out of the shower and Callie was going through my underwear drawer. I'm thinking again with the underwear? Liz goes She was holding the bras up to herself and looking in the mirror. It was eerie. I felt like the next thing she'd want was to crawl into my skin. I just told her then and there she'd gone too far and went cold turkey. I haven't seen her since. Dahlia, released by the inevitable end of a story about Callie, finally goes to get the dessert.

At least she stuck to your underwear Liz, excuse the imagery, I mean she could've decided to try on Stuart I say looking at Stuart. He shifts in his chair a bit and they don't look at each other. Uh oh. It never occurred to me that Callie would pounce on Stuart. I mean he's a sweet guy and all but I thought Callie had some scruples, even in her quantity phase. I never should've told her how many men I'd slept with. I look at Hugh thinking oops, like he can hear what I'm thinking. He's eating with his fork and fingers instead of his knife and I remember how much that annoyed me at the coop. It's annoying me now.

What did she want from us anyway? Hugh wants to know, like it just crossed his mind all of a sudden. Liz seems to have gotten to him. He's a bit flushed, a bit intense. After all these years I've never been able to figure that out he says regretfully. Oh who knows Hugh I say. Dahlia yells from the kitchen She was the most obsessed with you Becky because she never had you in the same way she did the rest of us. What are you telling us Dahl? Max wants to know. I don't like where this is going. But I can't figure out how to stop it. Dahlia sits down with new wine, goes No, no, I never slept with her, although we did come close. Liz goes Dahlia this isn't anything I really want to hear. For once I'm with Liz, but I would never say that. Well Liz you got your turn, now it's mine. Liz digs in, goes I'm very uncomfortable with this Dahlia. So you don't have to stay if you're uncomfortable. Dahlia's generous with the sick and feeble, which disqualifies Liz but probably not Stuart, but he's leaving with his wife anyway.

Liz is all stiff and straining at the door. Stuart gathers up their stuff and kisses Dahlia on the cheek and goes Sorry Dahlia, Becky. Dahlia goes Stuart you're welcome here any time. I purse my lips at him. See ya. He goes to Liz, hands her her bag, opens the door for her. I'm hoping he lets it slam on her, I'm hoping he stays. He doesn't.

Good riddance. Yeah really Max, she can't tell me to shut up in my own house and expect me to take it. You people are awfully volatile Hugh says looking nervous. How can you live this way, I'm exhausted. I go Yeah but Hugh, Liz is embalmed, if it weren't for Stuart, I mean at least she had the sense to marry someone who could keep her alive or a reasonable facsimile thereof. Max goes Blah blah who cares about Liz. I want to know why Dahlia didn't sleep with Callie. Dahlia goes

Get comfy. Like we could now. We stick the takeout cartons in the fridge in silence, take our wine into the livingroom. I watch Dahlia move with her dancerly grace, with her purpose. She won't look at me.

I sink into her chocolate silkcord couch, grab a suede pillow to hold, see myself reach for my wineglass in the giltedged mirror Dahlia has leaning against the biggest wall in her livingroom. The mirror makes me anxious. I watch myself in it, see that I'm looking way better than earlier, see the wineglow on my face, see the few remaining roses blooming in my hair, wait for everyone to sit down, watch them navigate in the mirrorworld, watch who will sit next to me. Dahlia sits on a big red pillow on the floor, her back straight against the wall. Max comes and lies down on the couch, puts his head on the pillow on my lap. Hugh looks perplexed at this but he won't do anything about it. He sits across from Dahlia, alone on an overstuffed ottoman, hugging himself a little. Dahlia goes Anybody have to pee? Max goes No Dahlia, we thought of that for ourselves already, you can start.

She does. It was a couple weeks after that last Christmas. She trails off, starts to twist her hair in her hands. Her voice warbles with embarrassment, the violence of forcing herself to tell. I'm hoping she changes her mind, spares herself, us. She has a different idea. Callie was out of her mind over falling out with Becky and she'd been calling me at least 4 times a day. I really felt sorry for her, not because Becky did anything wrong, she looks at me, but Callie was just so distraught. She'd say things like Why can't I keep people in my life? You're so good at that Dahlia, so many of your exlovers are still your friends. Hugh looks at Max. Max gives Hugh a gleeful little wave. Dahlia shakes her head at them, shakes them off, goes Callie was all, you know, I can't even keep my friends as friends. I told her You want too much from us Callie. You need too much that we just can't give you. You have to find it in yourself. She basically pleaded with me like How? like I could tell her how. I told her to go back to therapy, that she needed to take a hard look at herself and make some changes or she would never feel any different than she did right then. I really thought she might listen to me. You know how sometimes she was so lucid? I nod because she really could be, unpredictably she would do without her usual distortions. She said she'd think about it. She asked if she could stay with me for a little while, she was unbearably lonely, she kept saying Am I that unlovable? So I let her stay, her place was so small and dark and I thought a change of digs would do her good.

Dahlia leans forward, from her waist, crisscrosses her arms, grabs her toes. Her legs don't bend. She takes a deep diaphragm breath, releases her remembering. One night I came home. And the apartment was dark. Except for about a hundred candles around the room. Callie was where you are now Becky. Dahlia pauses again, exhales forcibly. She looks at me, goes Callie was masturbating. In front of my mirror. She looked up at me when I came in but she didn't stop touching herself. I was so stunned I just stood there. Callie had one of her breasts in her hand and her tongue was out, she was trying to lick her nipple, I mean she was trying to suck her own breast. I was a little bit sick to my stomach. I just shut down. I couldn't move I was so shocked. Callie looked at me and in this kind of bewildered way goes Dahlia why don't you help me with this. I somehow found my voice and said Callie, come on. She goes Just come here Dahl, it'll be good, I'm a really good lover. Dahlia looks shyly at Max and me. This may seem weird you guys but I sort of felt that everything had fallen into place, that maybe this was what it had been about between us all along, even my feelings for Max made more sense in that moment. She looks at Max like she's sorry. I see the top of Max's dark head, see his face disturbed in that mirror, hear Dahlia's voice shake. I remember thinking this was what my father's visitations had brought me to, and that I might feel safer with a woman. Even Callie. And she was so beautiful in that light, there were all these little candles twinkling around her and her reflection and then mine when I went to her. She put her hand up to my nose. She goes Wait till you taste it. I knew if I thought about it too long I'd change my mind and my rejection would totally crush her. I felt like the salve she needed.

I kissed her on that little mouth of hers, felt her tongue on mine, it was so soft. She started kissing me, taking off my clothes. I kissed her back, her face, her breasts, she wanted me to suck her. I started to but really ravenously. I wasn't doing it for her anymore. She held my head still all of a sudden, made me look at her eyes. You really want me, don't you. I nodded. And then she started to cry. I go What's wrong Callie? Her face was all bunching up and she goes I'm so sorry Dahlia, I just can't do this. What's the matter? The second I felt you wanting me it was like a switch flipped off inside me. It's not you, this happens every time I try to love someone. There's something wrong with me. The only way I can come is if I watch myself. I can usually go through the motions with a lover but with you I have to be honest Dahlia. It's just never as good as when I'm alone. She cried for like an hour. I just held her and watched her look at us in the mirror every now and then, like to make sure it was real. She left after that.

Max is up on his elbow, his worry for Dahlia propping him up. Hugh has his beard in his hands, he's looking at his shoes, rocking himself. No one says a word. We're all taking in Dahlia's portrait of Callie, absorbing it into our own ideas of her, of both of them. But I'm not surprised by Dahlia's story like Max and Hugh. I heard it before. From Callie. She sent me a letter, told me everything, pretty much exactly how Dahlia just did. Except she told me I was the one she really wanted. That wasn't the truth and I knew it. The only one Callie ever wanted was Callie.

CALLIE

She's standing in front of a golden mirror, her elbow angled up, her long arm wrapped around the back of her dark head, her hand pulling her hair away from her pale face. She's trying to see her own profile, trying to know what she looks like when she doesn't know she's being looked at. She shifts her glance to me, lets her hair fall, doesn't turn away from the mirror, says You can touch me if you want.

I force myself awake. I look around, feel the lush, strange sheets, the warmth another body has left in the bed next to me. All at once I know where I am. In Dahlia's bed, it smells clean like her. I struggle between wanting to find her and wanting to linger here, with the remnant of her scent. I close my eyes.

The aroma of coffee stirs me, revives me from drifting. It smells like safety. I open my eyes and see Hugh with a tray, the coffee, a cutopen grapefruit. This little still life means Dahlia's in the kitchen, directing the nourishment of her friends. Of me. Today's your big day Sleeping Beauty. Hugh is smiling, jarring, I'd managed to forget everything in sleep. Hugh's jolted me back to my recent state of anxious knowledge. Where's Max? I'm not sure why I asked this, except the gang's all here, and I haven't had any coffee so I'm incompetent. Plus I want to know. I watch my question strike Hugh's whole body, regret it. He had some stuff to do Hugh says dejectedly, slumping into himself. He deposits the tray at my feet, starts to shrink away. I moan Hugh. Yeah? he says all hopeful. His eyes are deeply green and needy. I try to think of an apology, can't, feel the silence weighing on us, think an apology would make it worse. Nevermind. He turns away from me, leaves me alone. He goes to Dahlia.

I hear their breakfast sounds down the hall, the scratch of a fork on ceramic, the murmur of low talking. I wonder who's confiding in whom. Whose need is greater? Whose pressing urgency to spill their guts over what gnaws at them, Dahlia's over Callie or Hugh's over me.

I should go and try to mend the fence Hugh and I have broken sitting on it too long.

I fling the sheet off me, feel the air rush to my body, feel it arouse me, wake me up. The light in Dahlia's bedroom is so soft, so warm, so strawcolored as it hits my skin. I wonder what Hugh would think if he came back here right now, what he would see. A body, well proportioned, slightly excited, ready to feel. I'm like a Kodacolor cutout of myself glued to the soft canvas of Dahlia's sheet. What would it feel like to be painted on, to let a cool, wet brush glide over me, layer me in thick, rich paint, in color beyond what I'm capable of through blush of shame or excitement. I roll around in my luxury, run my body over Dahlia's sheets. Where does she buy these? They must cost a bundle. More than I can afford on nothing a year.

Hugh and Dahlia are loading the dishwasher. They're still talking, low and serious. Talking to each other won't solve their problems. They're going about it all wrong, all indirectly. Max would never resort to mutual woundlicking. He used to get so mad at Callie's selfpityfests. She couldn't go through them alone, tried to drag him in, drag him down. That's what he told me.

We'd spent one of our endless Sundays at Cafe Colonial reading the whole Times, having our coffeecups perpetually refilled. Except Dahlia. Max and Callie'd managed to get to the point where they could be in the same room together after the Max and Dahlia debacle. We'd get the big table by the window and hog it for hours. We only got kicked out like twice for loitering. Mostly we read, but when Callie was in a mood she'd monopolize us, anyone who'd listen. A few weeks straight she'd been raving over some new guy she was seeing, the dentist. The chiropractor. No, the dentist. So that morning she came late, her face a big blotch. Well, it's over. Already? Max couldn't stifle his spitetinged merriment over her getting dumped so soon. She was pouting, telling Dahlia and me that the dentist had dumped her the day after the first time they slept together. What kind of creep does that? she wanted to know.

Max stopped smirking, stopped listening. But when he'd gotten through Sunday Styles, Arts and Leisure, The City, Sports, and Automobiles, in that order, always in that order, he started to pay attention again. Callie was still whining, watching herself in the glass tabletop, the window, Dahlia's eyes, mine. And when Max let her have it it was ugly. Oh Callie grow up. When are you gonna realize that it's really a downer that all you have to talk about is how rotten men are to you, and now for the real revelation, there are other people in the universe and we're not all interested in every excruciating detail of your selfindulgent suffering. I thought Callie would smack him, I thought she should. She just sat there, puffylipped, thoughtful, like she was trying to figure out how to kill Max. And maybe the dentist too. And maybe every man she'd ever met in her entire life. And then she looked up at him with a hint of a smile in her eyes and said You're right Max. I'm sorry I was so thoughtless. It must be very difficult for you to hear about my lovers. Max's mouth opened but before any sound came out Callie goes Oh and Max. Fuck you. He just rolled his eyes, got up, threw some money on the table, and headed for the door. Everyone was staring. I couldn't stand it anymore, I finally said Just sit down Max. No more scenes you guys alright? But he's the one Knock it off Callie. Either we sit here and pretend we're civilized or I'm leaving and I'll never speak to either of you again, your call. Max actually sat down, surprised by my ultimatum.

So we made it through one more blowout but then Max and I got left alone the last few blocks home. Big mistake. Becky why do you of all people put up with that poor me drivel? That's one of the million reasons I left her, she was so depressing sometimes. I mean how much of her shit can you let her dump on you before you're buried? Not only did I loathe his imagery, I was irritated that he just couldn't let it go. All I could think to say was Well Max I guess I have more ego strength than you. He stopped walking, his elbows raised up like he might start flapping. He put his hands on his hips. You know what Becky? What? Max. You're as fucked up as she is. Oh how would you know Max, you don't know the first thing about me. I know you need to surround yourself with weak links so you can feel superior. Right Max. And you're Johnny Depp.

I pass the diningtable, gather up a couple of wine-stained glasses as an offering, enter the kitchen ready to help. Dahlia and Hugh are bent over the dishwasher, rearranging splotchy plates to make things fit. Hugh notices me. He eyes Dahlia. They ignore me. I feel the urge to butt their heads together and watch the stars twitter above them. I go You know what? They say What? at the same time, looking up at me reluctantly. I'm sorry I've been so selfabsorbed and thoughtless, but you guys are acting like victims, and you better get over it before tonight or you know Callie's gonna smell it on you and this whole plan will be a complete waste of energy. They look at each other, grudgingly nodding. I hand them the wineglasses and go back to bed.

I look in the mirror, see if I need a slip under this dress, do, don't want to wear one, slips make me feel like I'm

10 or a librarian. I throw the dress on the floor. Dahlia indulges me, hands me a pink thing I would never wear even though I love the color. I try it on anyway. To please Dahlia. I look sweet, nice, defenseless. No way Dahl. Oh come on, do the AntiBlack thing Becky. Everyone always wears black to openings. Dahlia, there will be 6 large collages of me naked, I do not need to be calling any more attention to myself by wearing pink. So show me what you've got in black or let me go home and find something in my own closet. Oh Beck. She holds the pink dress up to herself. How bout if I wear it then. I'm thinking great, a 6foot beauty in pink will steal all the attention from me. Maybe the pressure too. Yeah Dahl, that's perfect. Now give me all your blacks. Go Fish she says over her shoulder as she glides to her huge walkin closet in her giant bedroom.

I'm left, naked, in front of that mirror. I look at myself, shudder, feel the sadness of Callie's failures, feel how utterly alone she must have felt, always, how stuck inside herself. I feel a twinge of guilt over our petty revenge plan, think how stupid it is, how off target, how too late, how redundant to punish Callie, but I'm completely fascinated by what she might have become. I want to see her. I want her to come.

She'll walk into the gallery, big and pale and captivating. She'll grab a glass of wine, apply it to that little mouth of hers, walk around sipping, looking at my pieces, eyes wide, blown away. She'll be moved, nostalgic, wondering what I'm like now, wondering where I am. She'll look around, see me, see me looking fantastic, clothed in Dahliablack, in admiration. I'll be talking to someone, a magazine person, giving an interview about my themes, my form, my content. Callie will notice, hover, eavesdrop, wait till she can have my undivided attention. She'll hug me, tell me she's missed me, tell me she's sorry, tell me she's changed. She's luminous, she owns the room, and all she wants is forgiveness. From me.

Dahlia comes back with hangers in both hands, black drapey things streaming from them. She's generous, doesn't bring me her B list stuff, gives me everything she's got. She can, she can trust me, I'm not Callie. Callie borrowed a Romeo Gigli, she loved the black lace bodice, loved how it looked against what she called the porcelain of her skin. She was too big for it, too big-breasted, but she closed herself into it anyway, wore it on a first date with some investment banker, to a fundraiser, brought it back shredded at the seams, the silk threads burst against her body. Callie cried when Dahlia noticed. Dahlia told me. Dahlia shrugged it off, said

Callie's selfimage was distorted, that was her excuse for Callie, that's why Dahlia forgave her.

I put something on before I say So are you ok about last night? about telling us what happened with you and Callie? Her arms drop and the black droops on the floor. Yeah, it was hard but I really felt I needed to tell you guys. There's nothing more painful than a festering secret. Plus I think I didn't want Callie to have anything over me when we see her, especially something so humiliating. If she'd told you guys about that night instead of me she would've won.

I'm so glad Dahlia doesn't know I knew, so glad I can shield her from this degradation at least, so happy I held my tongue, a little sick about it, a little afraid. I didn't say anything to Dahlia when I got Callie's letter thinking Dahlia would confide it. But sooner. Way sooner. I didn't say anything to Dahlia last night. No one did. What could we say. We all just went to her, held her. Dahlia would be so defeated if she knew Callie had sent me that horrible letter.

Or would she. I feel a vibration deep inside me, a rumbling of now or never, this is my chance, I should come clean, tell Dahlia right this second so it never comes between us. I look up at her, her beautiful blacks still, limp on the floor, her eyes looking down at them, not seeing. How much can one person deal with at once.

Maybe I should wait. I'll get another chance to tell her. What good would it do now? It's not like Callie's gonna show up, if she shows at all, and the first words out of her mouth will be to tell Dahlia this one thing. It can wait.

I pick the hems up off the floor, say How bout this one Dahl? Sure Beck. Excellent choice she says with fake enthusiasm. But she snaps out of her daze. Let me show you how to wear it. I watch her big hands work the gauzy dress off its silkquilted hanger. I feel funny watching them, shy, I try not to think of them touching Callie, of Dahlia wanting her. Uh, you'll have to take that one off first Beck. I'm just standing here like an idiot, watching her be gentle with the dress, with me. Becky you can't wear both these dresses at a time no matter how badly you want to hide. It's your day. People will be there to see you and you have to let them look. Oh God Dahl, I'm dysfunctional. Come on Becky, let me babysit you today, you might go play in traffic or something. What about Hugh? He can babysit you tomorrow. Funny Dahl, I mean what's he Where I'm taking you Hugh can't go.

Dahlia stops in front of Inkspot Tattoo. I picture her holding me down while some guy with hair growing out of the purple dragon on his shoulder tries to stick the

Mona Lisa under my skin. Dahlia I really don't think Wait right here Becky. She walks to A, hails a cab, goes Get in. I do. Prince and Broadway please. Where are you taking me Dahl? You'll see. Just sit back and relax. Easy for you to say Dahlia. Yeah yeah tell me all about it, you think I don't get stagefright? Yeah but when you're dancing you're a moving target. I on the other hand have to enclose myself in a little room and let people tell me their opinions to my face. The cabdriver looks in his rearview mirror at us, like to see if we're famous. I'm not saying what you do is easy Dahlia, but you just have to do your work and wait for the applause to kinda waft over you. There's something about people putting their applause or lack thereof into words that's more pointed, more scary than primitive noise. Or even silence. I guess I never thought about it like that Beck. But you're right, the times I've been reviewed I had to deal with whatever that person wrote about me instead of being left to imagine what the audience meant by their clapping.

She looks out the window like she's picturing herself onstage, like she's reliving being praised, admired, loved. She deserves that. More than anyone. I wish she'd perform more often. She hardly ever wants to. I watch her reveling, watch the East Village whizz by beside her, notice Callie's block as we pass it, see Dahlia notice it. Think she'll come Becky? Not if she has any sense.

I smell oleander. That would be the oleander Becky, it's in the mud. We're up to our necks in it, our faces caked with sludge, our eyes covered with cucumbers. I'm holding a freezing glass of limey water in my hand, afraid to set it down blindly, afraid I'm an accident waiting to happen.

So Becky, what's up with you and Hugh? Nothing. No change. Well, I think I can tell you without betraying any confidence that he's totally confused about you, you're giving him mixed signals you know. I picture myself as a traffic light, red and green. I wait for the light to change. It doesn't. You know I love Hugh, I just don't have the energy right now to figure out what to do about him. I mean it might be different if we'd slept together on Wrap Awareness Night but you know, between my show and your little Callie scheme I'm beyond making decisions at the moment and I definitely don't want to run any red lights. Huh? The point is Dahl, can you see Hugh living in New York? She doesn't answer, then goes It would devour him wouldn't it. Exactly. He may be some corporate raider finance guy in Sunnyvale but he wouldn't last a second in this town. So you've never thought about going back to California Beck? Have you? No. Exactly. Why would we? All our stuff's here.

One of my cucumbers falls and out one eye I see Dahlia grinning. How often do you do this Dahl? Spa? Yeah. Like once a week. Man, I'd be a total slug if I stayed this relaxed all the time. Good, so it's working. I raise my hand out of the muck, feel like a total bottom-dweller, feel for my cucumber, put it back on my eye. You know how many extra coffees I'm gonna have to drink just to break even today? I wish you wouldn't drink so much of that stuff, it's bad for you. It's not so bad. Oleander's poison if you eat it but that doesn't stop you from immersing yourself in it once a week. It's exactly the same thing, I use coffee therapeutically. Right Beck, when we're 40 you're gonna be all fibroidy and wish you'd listened to me. When we're 40 Dahlia I'll be a famous artist and come here once a day and be as healthy as you. It doesn't work like that Becky. Your body's a fragile ecosystem and dunking yourself in nature even once a day isn't gonna fix the damage all that caffeine's doing to it. When something upsets the balance, the whole ecosystem suffers. Dahlia? Yeah? I thought you brought me here to get me in a tensionfreezone. Sorry Becky. Alright, I'll nag you tomorrow. Want some more water? Sure. I hear some gritty movement from her mudvat. Where's that damned bell?

The gallery looks good. On the left wall are Lips Stick and Wet Dream. On the right are See Through and Object of Desire. Straight on is I of the Beholder, and around the corner, in its own little room which was built to convey the wrong impression of a series of galleries, hangs Monumental Vanity.

I am way early. The invitations say 6. It's 5:50. Maya has me hiding in her office so I can make some kind of an entrance at the appointed, fashionably late hour of 6:40, like I'm too busy to go to my own opening. The office is dark, hot. I pace, eat my nails, wait for Maya to bring red wine. You get one glass now and one to walk around with. Period. Keep your wits about you, your wit, be amusing, someone important might show. Yes, someone important. I wonder what she looks like, what she's doing, under whose influence she's finding herself.

I check the little mirror in Maya's closet every 5 minutes. I look good in Dahlia's sheer LeFay but I can't resist the urge to make sure. I'm too nervous. Not about my work. My work's good. Maya greeted me with a smile and much arm touching. She said Becky you do not disappoint.

I check my watch. 6:10. No one will show till 6:15 at the earliest. Max and Dahlia and Hugh will show at 6:30, they promised. Callie may or may not show. If she doesn't I will have had an excellent distraction from worrying over the artworld turnout. If she shows, she'll see me as I want her to, happy, mildly successful on my way to more, surrounded by my friends who love me and not her.

She will also see me naked. As will a roomful of people. Some of them may print me naked in their magazines. Some may take me naked home. If I'm lucky. What the hell was I thinking? I'm wearing this glorious dress and they'll all be looking right through it. How could I not have realized this out of my mind moment would come, that I'd have to go out there, make my entrance, face those people, see them looking at me. I'm insane. I want to run out there before a crowd forms, rip the collages off the walls, wreck my precious edges, wrap the canvases around me, run out the frontdoor. The headlines will read Artist Selfdestructs. Collagist Collapses. Portraitist Pukes. Neofigurativist Has Nervous Breakdown. Maybe I should. You can't buy that kind of press.

I look in the mirror again. I don't look worried.

It's time. Finally. Maya will be coming for me. I jump up and down a few times to see my figure in the tiny mirror. I've been living on coffee for so many weeks I'm actually too thin. Maybe people will think that's not my body in the collages, that I did a Hoch and used remnant nudes, or that I hired a model, grafted her body beneath my head. Who would know but Dahlia. And Hugh. They wouldn't contradict me. I could tell people that. I could.

Maya slithers in, takes my hand, pulls me out of her office, into a crowd. The first person I see is Dahlia, beaming, rosy. She's standing near Wet Dream with Hugh who looks dorky in his blazer and embarrassed by my work but he smiles anyway. I hope no one mistakes him for my lover. Max walks up to them carrying wine and they say something to him and he looks over at me, puts his glass in his teeth, gives me silent applause. I'm so grateful he's primitive. Maya drags me toward a very tanned guy with platinum hair. I look over my shoulder to give my pals a mockhelpless shrug but they're not looking my way.

Everyone else is. They're staring at me, wondering about me, comparing me to my work, like we're the same. Then I see myself as they do and we are the same, naked, exposed to these strangers, their curiosity, their take. I have opened myself up to their interpretation of me, their shared meaning. But my pieces aren't all that I am. They're the extreme me, the me that tries to be fearfree, boundaryfree, by existing for at least one brief moment on the edge, the edge of limits, of comfort, of obscenity, of acceptability. Of eroticism and taboo and death. I want to avenge the human condition, make up for how small we are, life is, how short, how sad, how painful. I hear obvious students earnestly discussing the symbolism of the black velvet ribbon around my neck in I of the Beholder. She's referencing Manet's Olympia. How do you know she's not referencing Kahlo's selfreference, a ribbon around a bomb? I wonder how this guy means bomb. Other blackclad spectators comment, their voices reach me in gushes of opinion. These represent 20th century disconnection. These are erotic. Yeah, autoerotic. I've turned everyone in this room into a voyeur. Of life beyond the ordinary. It's thrilling.

I wonder if I've done this to my friends. I seek them out, their reactions, can't wait to hear what Max will say now that he's free to say it. I spot them, huddled together at the wine table. I move toward them, tingling, anticipating and scared, hoping they will love the me in my work, hoping they will really know me and survive the knowledge. If they don't, if they can't, then I really am alone, without family, what has passed for it.

There's Terri from The Archive heading me off, coming to keep me from them, smiling. Becky. Hi Terri. Becky this is my boyfriend Ted. Yeah, hi Ted, I remember you from the holiday party. Hi he chokes out, his eyes straying around my dress, the worm. I want to take him by the shoulders and shake him and yell at him Don't be so literal! and by extension alert the whole room. Terri notices Ted's glancing and goes Uh, this is powerful stuff. Yeah? I smile at her, knowing she will shake Ted. I'm ignoring Ted, now and forever. Eli's supposed to be coming, have you seen him yet? I look around the room for our boss who always promises, rarely delivers. Nope, no sign of him. Terri has nothing else to say to me and I try to figure out how to get away. I gaze longingly at the wine table, say I need a drink, be right back. My little gang is still hovering there.

Behind them, all alone, a woman who sort of looks like Callie, tall, darkhaired, very pale, moves toward them. They don't see her yet but I do. It has to be her. She's fixed on them, directed at them. She doesn't see me. I can't get there in time to see if it's really her, to warn them, oh god it is her! to hear her first words to them, to see her reaction to our lame attempt to prove we don't need her. Maya latches on to me, leads me around the room like a showdog, makes me shake hands with people, roll over, speak, respond to the witty things she's saying. I'm meeting people I should care about meeting and all I can do is wonder what Callie will say. To me. Maya goes Uh Becky, you could do that, right? prompting me to tune in or at least pretend I'm paying attention to this guy in a very nice suit who wants something from me. I wonder what. Sure, you'll arrange it for me won't you Maya? She looks surprised as her head nods. I take the guy's hand and lean toward his ear like I'm telling him a secret. You wouldn't believe how Maya spoils me. He goes I'm sure you deserve it. He's still holding my hand. The last thing I want is to have to shake off someone important to my career. But Callie's here. I slide my hand away, run it through my hair. I smile at them and make like I'm going for wine and Maya lets me off my leash.

As I get closer I look above the crowd for Dahlia who always towers. She and Max and Hugh and Callie are nestled near See Through and I cut through the little groups of gawkers toward them. Then I hear it, Callie's laugh, and I can't get there fast enough. All these people in the room, they know who I am, hands grab mine, pat my back, strangers go Wow, nice work, You're brave, What made you think of that? I'm barely polite, say Yeah, glad you came, say Thanks, say Excuse me, say

Can I get through? The buzz in the room gets quieter when I pass, people look at me like I'm a big deal because I take naked pictures of myself, because I cut them up, because I paint, because I glue, because it occurred to me and not them that this is a great way to spend time, to make a living, to become known, at least in the tiny universe of this room, I'm huge.

I don't like it. I don't like their greedy wondering eyes on me. I don't want this much attention. I want to be standing with Callie who could always suck up the attention in a room, like she went around with a big invisible straw sucking, sucking till there was no more attention left to take, and she just kept on till her sucking made a sound like a kid at the end of a milkshake. If I had a straw I'd be blowing into it, I'd put the end of my straw into hers and blow and she'd suck up all the attention I can't handle, all of it.

I'm in range. I could splash my wine right into Max's face and he wouldn't even notice because Callie's here. I could take off all my clothes and cover myself in Saran Wrap and Hugh's gaze would not be diverted because Callie's here. I could scream at the top of my lungs Dahlia I knew all about your temptation in the mirror and my voice wouldn't reach her. Callie's here. She's laughing. She's got the floor. She's got my friends and they're happy she's here. And when she sees me, she holds their attention, turns her own on me like a hose and I step back with the force of it. Callie. Becky. She leans toward me, kisses my cheek, smiles, says Thanks for asking me, in a normal tone of voice, in English, she kisses my other cheek, holds my arms, looks at me. You look incredible Becky. I feel incredible, absolutely amazing. Like I matter, like I'm the only one who does.

Dahlia goes Becky doesn't Callie look beautiful? All I can say is Of course like Dahlia's an imbecile. Hugh goes She's teaching now, special ed for mentally retarded kids. Developmentally disabled Callie corrects. Hugh blushes and goes Right, sorry. He hates being corrected. Precision's his only real passion.

Callie's eyes return to me. They always do. I fix on her hair, flash on how she used to come out of her shower, wetheaded, dripping, holding her mother's mother of pearl comb which she'd hand me, turning her back to me, looking at me over her shoulder without saying a word. I'd comb straight down her back and she'd shiver and say That's so nice Becky. But that's all gone, cut short. How a schoolteacher would wear it. At least it covers those big ears of hers. She's clenching my invitation, it's crumpled in her hand, just enough of Lips Stick visible, red and ghoulblue, it looks like a poison apple.

I say So you're still on East 5th. Yep, that old apartment I got with Max. He goes That was a sweet little place. Dahlia goes Yeah it was. Funny how we're all delusional. That place was a dive. But we all lived in it. Except Hugh who was only a memory to Callie. Remember when we painted my brick wall black Becky? I remember. I remember how I brought bagels and she made coffee in her French carafe and we sat around talking until it was too dark to see and she finally noticed and pulled herself away from me to go turn on the light. I remember that we used brushes instead of rollers to get in the brick cracks but it took way long and we opened a bottle of wine and ended up calling her mother to ask for money which we planned to spend on more wine, better wine. And hair care products. I remember that she offered me her shower and I took it and put on her black robe and felt its silky smoothness on mine and I didn't know what she wanted from me but all it was was to be with me, to see what would happen between us, what we would talk about, what we would invent together. I remember the thrill of her attention. It returns to me again and again. She's trying to reconnect, to rejoin me, to belong with me. Is it still black? Yeah, I never got around to repainting it but it got to feeling pretty dark in there so I hung a big mirror on it.

Even the creepiness of this revelation and all that it implies doesn't break the amnesia bubble I've blown over myself. I want to forget her desperation. Or I want it not to matter. It doesn't matter. Some people are worth the trouble they put you through. Some people make you feel alive by their ferocious example. Some people have the nerve to be as sick as they are. Some people are as brave as Callie. She wants therefore she is.

I go You look really good Callie and she does. Pale as ever, she looks clean and new, like she deserves her freckles, the innocence they portend. Becky she says, my name in her mouth, in the space between us. How bout showing me the rest of the show? Sure. We don't move, the others won't let us, they stop us with their groupness, their reluctance to let us go.

Callie goes This is a pretty strange little reunion isn't it? Max goes Only if you think about it. Max is right. He's doing what I'm doing. He's living in the moment, enjoying himself, enjoying Callie. I look at Hugh who's not saying much, except with his body. He's all crimped, he's hugging his blazer, he's hugging his injury over what to call Callie's students, over his inability to hold on to Callie so long ago, to hold her attention. My attention. That's how he is, determined to stay unworthy, he's holding himself back, he's standing real close to Dahlia, like she can protect him. I wonder how Dahlia thinks her revenge plan is going, she's chatting happily, blissfully along with everyone else, no scratching out of eyes, no crying and screaming at each other, no scene. No revenge. Callie seems calm, relieved we're not gonna dis her. We didn't even plan to, really, our plan never got that far, our plan never got beyond the frontdoor of the gallery. I wonder if this was our plan all along. To get her back. I wonder if we couldn't get along without her. Callie's looking at me, eyes bright, expectant.

How bout that tour? I feel her hand on my back, feel the confidence of her pushing, her choosing me, steering me away from my little gang.

Becky. I haven't seen your work in a long, long time. You've really blossomed, you kept at it, I admire that. I wish I had that kind of staying power. I can't really do anything else Callie. What about The Archive? Yeah, I'm still there, I just don't consider it any great contribution to humanity matching pictures to magazine covers or ad copy, not like teaching disadvantaged kids, when did you start doing that? About a year ago. After you guys dropped me I felt like such a loser for having screwed up so many good friendships. I went back to therapy and did a lot of soul searching.

I search her eyes, the sapphire studs in her face that

shine and dazzle and deflect my attempt to see her core. I search her voice for recrimination, for blame, for hurt, for anger and hear none. So that really turned things around for you? Yeah, that and a ton of Prozac. She's laughing at herself but she gets serious fast. I was a mess for a long time Becky. I couldn't understand why I was so empty, why I'd been so thoroughly rejected by you guys. I keep saying you guys but I mean you Becky. She touches my arm, says my name too much, like she's been longing to say it. You're the one I missed. I always wanted to be like you, you're so smart and brave and talented, all the things I always wished I was, I mean just look at these pictures. You have something to say and you just do it. So when you cut me off I thought if I changed you'd care about me again. Or that I would.

All this time and she's still holding on to whatever it was that we were to each other. A bad accident that Hugh caused, caused me, caused Dahlia, even Max. And do you? Do I care about myself? She laughs quietly, goes I guess I'm still working on that. First I had to forgive myself for all the revolting stuff I did. And said. That took quite a few sessions, as you might imagine. She touches my hand, laughs again. I'm wondering if she let herself off easy. Then came the really hard stuff Becky, the digging down deep. I'm wondering how much she really agonized. I missed a lot as a kid, the most obvious thing being a father. I never wanted to admit it, that not knowing my father had any effect on me at all. That was wishful thinking, clearly.

I'm thinking she's saying all the right things, and I want to believe them, believe her. But I'm getting this icky feeling that whoever this is standing next to me, this person who basically traumatized 4 people, at least, this woman who existed by virtue of her audacity, this so-called friend who put me on some pedestal just so she could knock me off it, she's different in the wrong way, selfconsciously sick instead of free.

You know Becky, the whole time I was in therapy I thought about you, you're still my hero. Her voice goes a little brittle, and I'm not sure what's scarier, the thought that redeeming herself with me will make up for everything she ever fucked up in her life or the thought that maybe she needs a lot more than Prozac to live as her painful self or the thought that she's lying and she really wants something from me besides to save her. I'm a little claustrophobic all of a sudden. I don't want to be her hero. I go Isn't that some kind of displacement thing Callie, isn't that what your therapist is for? Or your mother? I wish. My mom's still roving from one man to the next and that's even more pathetic at 50 than it was at 30. She watches herself say this in the reflection of the window.

The old dread dredges itself up in me. I am happy to see her, I mean I was, but the thought of starting up with her again exhausts me. I just look at her. If I could figure out a way to sniff her fingers nonchalantly I'd know if she's really changed.

Becky you don't know how hard it was for me to come. Her big eyes are tearful, trying to see into me, which makes me want to hide, to run. I go I do know Callie, I'm really glad you did. She smiles, her eyelashes bat back her tears. But I'm not really looking for any new and improved you. Her smile evaporates but I have to finish. I guess I felt bad that everything got so ugly between us but to be honest it's just been easier without you. She takes in a quick little breath. I take her hand. I don't mean to be mean, I'm just explaining my feelings then. You were such an important part of my life, I mean if it wasn't for you I might not have come to New York. She squeezes my hand. But you were too intense Callie, you took so much energy. I couldn't do it anymore.

What about now? she wants to know. A little too desperate. I still have her hand, I don't know what to do with it. Pat it? Press it against my cheek and inhale? I let it go. She wraps it around my arm. I feel like a prize. I feel like an idiot in the long tense pause I've created. I feel stuck. I look around for Maya, see if she's looking for me. All I see is a crowded room, people drinking wine, gossiping, talking about me, my work. Or maybe not. Maybe my work's just a freedrink backdrop, something to do on a Thursday night, a place to be seen. It's not about me at all, it's not about art. I haven't goaded anyone into considering nakedness versus nudity, redefining seen and seer, I haven't inspired anyone to think about containment, about what is and is not solipsism, confessional art. The only person in the room who's telling me I've provoked anything is Callie.

Callie. I feel helpless, take a long, strengthening breath. I dig down deep, to find a way out, to wipe her filmy feelings off me, to put them back on her. A million moments with Callie jam my confused brain and all I feel is hard, hardened. Realistically Callie, after all that's happened, what do you think we can be to each other? She flushes, all the way down to her chest, her eyes begin to sparkle. She faces me, clutches my arm with both her hands. Oh Becky I just want you to care about me like you used to. Is that impossible? Of course it is I want to say, I can't erase the Callie I know, the too many Callies in all their gritty realism, all their need and want. I stall. I'm acting like I'm thinking hard about her question, I walk her around to avoid having to focus. She's watching my face, I feel like the next words out of my mouth could undo all the therapy and mood chemistry she's subjected herself to. We wander into the fake next gallery, round the corner to Monumental Vanity. Callie has her shoulder to it and I get the chills, her impossible question, the way her head turns awkwardly toward my collage, the way she looks back at me like I just pushed her off a cliff. She drops her glass, wine splashes my leg, Dahlia's gauze. Goddamn you Becky. What? I follow her eyes, wonder why she's cursing me when I haven't said a word, see her gaping at my collage. And then I see what I never saw before, until I turned the corner with her, until now. The black hair. The spattered freckles. The hands that hover awkwardly over the crotch. The frame of gilt. How could you! she screams. I'm all tense, shaky with fear, with consciousness. The other 3 people in this part of the gallery are looking at us, at the winesplatter, at the broken glass on the pristine floor, at my collage. They don't see the resemblance between Callie and the image it contains. But Callie does. And so do I.

She pushes me roughly as she runs away, into the main gallery. I go after her, not running, trying to look like my unconscious hasn't done something terrible, like I haven't been the epitome of passive aggression, like I haven't shown her at her most repulsive. My AntiVenus, my portrait of Callie in the mirror with a hundred candles twinkling. Only I'm Callie in the portrait, I made myself into her, took her worst self on, which doesn't seem to matter, she's still storming out.

I push past the slugs getting sloshed and checked out, reach the center of the gallery, smack into Maya who looks sorry she didn't keep me in tow. What was that all about? Nothing Maya, don't worry, just a friend. I'm hardly worried Becky, a little drama's good for business.

I brush her off, move through Callie's wake, see her near the front desk, surrounded by my friends, see them listening to her, see her head bent to cry, see Dahlia put her arm around her, turn to look at me, confused, Dahlia! I want to shout. Callie breaks free of Dahlia and rushes out the door. I watch as Max puts his hand on Hugh's back and Dahlia's, pushes them toward the door, watch as Hugh looks back at me, shaking his head, watch as they all walk out on me. I notice the crowd looking at me, through me, I notice I'm standing very still, in the middle of the hush in the room, utterly alone.

MAX

Hugh isn't coming back. I've been pawing his sweaters and luggage tags since the gallery closed 5 hours ago, willing him to walk through my door. It's not working. Nothing is. Not willing him to come to me, not hoping I haven't lost him. Not wanting him in the least.

I sit in my boudoirchair, Hugh's stuff at my feet, the phone in my lap, warm from my obsessive dialing. I've called Dahlia 42 times. She won't answer. Her mechanical command to speak cannot induce me to beg Please pick up Dahlia.

Max's machine isn't even on. Maybe he doesn't even

have one. How would I know, I never call him. Unless it's an emergency.

This is an emergency. It's 2am and all I can do is blast Bessie Smith, raise the arm on my turntable, play After You've Gone over and over, listen deeply to my pain, let her sing it, hear her do chiaroscuro better than anyone, wait for the neighbors to complain.

Where are my friends? I can just see them all together somewhere, running up Dahlia's gold card at my expense. Dahlia knows I knew what happened between her and Callie all along, long before she confessed. She knows I kept it from her, undermined her. She and Callie and Hugh and Max are huddled in some restaurant booth, talking about me, my treachery, my betrayal. What I've done outhurts anything Callie ever did, to any of us.

How could I have been so oblivious? How could I not have seen what I was doing when I picked up my brush and started flinging candlelight onto the canvas? All I know is Callie hasn't changed, she's as sharp as ever, her intuition, her fierce selfprotection, her selfimportance. Who else would've made the connection, who else would've assumed my selfportrait could be about her. If only I could've denied it, could've called her paranoid. If only I hadn't consented to my guilt.

This is Dahlia's fault. If she hadn't hatched this asinine plan in the first place Callie never would've seen the offending collage at all. She never would've known what I'd done. None of us would. It would've stayed some sublimated nightmare in which I'm pathetically Callie. I might not've even made the fucking piece if I hadn't been so freaked over the prospect of seeing her.

I wonder what she said to Dahlia to get her to abandon me at my show. I wonder what she's saying to them all right now. She wouldn't have to say much. I so fucked up. And Callie knows how to move them, how to wield her victimhood. All she has to do is cry and they're all in her pocket. She's the injured party, the victim of me, my fickle friends vying to prop her up. I picture Callie on 3 crutches named Dahlia, Max, and Hugh, I picture kicking them out from under her.

How can they fall for her again? They all saw through her once, how can they let themselves be conned, be convinced, be connived back into her fuckedup life? Max was right, they're weak, all of them, they'd rather be needed, cried into feeling healthy by contrast. They don't get that from me. I stand on my own. I'm the strong one. I make them feel inadequate, I know I do, but I can't help it, it's not my fault. I'm a survivor. Am I supposed to pretend I'm weaker than I am? Am I supposed to fake needing them in some way I don't? Isn't it enough that I like them, that I encourage them, that I'm honest with them, want to share my life with them? Isn't it enough that we've made each other family? That we've chosen each other again and again all these years, been more important than anyone else to each other? Or was the core of our friendship actually hollow, the void of Callie that made us cling to each other because we knew her like no one else did, because we cast her out. Because we survived her.

I can't stay sticking sweatily to my phone, I'm going nuts, can't sit still, can't stop dialing. But there's no one left to call. How did I become the persona non grata among us? A few strokes of my paintbrush.

I need to work, wet a brush and let go. I need to be painting anything. I go to my closet, fling open the doors, take down my paint, take down my brushes. There's no fucking canvas, I used it up. I ransack my apartment. No paper except news. No cardboard, no plywood, no cloth but my clothes. I back away from my closet, fling myself on my bed, look at the paintbrush in my hand, paint the air. Hear Bessie Smith. After you've gone and left me crying after you've gone there's no denying you'll feel blue you'll feel sad you'll miss the best friend you've ever had There'll come a time now

don't forget it there'll come a time when you'll regret it
I spring from my bed, calmed, brush in hand, move
toward the music, toward my turntable, toward my livingroom, look out my windows, wonder where they are,
my friends. Mine.

I go to the paint. See the tubes almost empty. Start
with black, match my mood, my soul, if I had one,
squeeze it out, onto my brush, brush the paint into a circle on my wall, paint another, the center, connect the
circles with spokes, 1, 2, 3. I stand there, look at it, jab at
it, blot it out. I've made a mess, I wallow in it, revel in
it, make it grow, watch my strokes fly, sure and violent,
see them sing, loud, flat, hear myself breathe hard, feel
myself sweat fast. My arm hurts, twinges, swings itself
down. I pull back, look coolly, see the swirling painted
wall, see the whirling black void, see what I've done, a
portrait of us. If Dahlia, Max, and Hugh are the spokes,
who's the hub and who's the rim?

I bundle up, fish the quarters from the pockets in my
closet, wish I had a cellphone, hate my building for having long corridors, pace the elevator, hate it for slowing
me down, hit the street finally, feel the cool air chill my
cheeks, walk toward Dahlia's, stop at the payphone on A

that's taunting me, dial Dahlia. Hi, This is Dahlia, leave a mes I hang up on her fucking machine, call Max, hear the ringing in my ear. It doesn't stop. I stop. Why am I doing this? They're the ones avoiding me. They're the ones forgetting what she's like, what I'm like, what our friendship's meant for all these years. They're the ones who'll suffer, they'll blow me off and hang with her till she screws them over again. It's inevitable. Then they'll realize it wasn't my fault, I didn't hurt her on purpose, I was just working through Callie in my own way. I never punished them for how they tried to get over her. I was there for them. I was their friend.

Big fucking deal if they never call me again. They're more trouble than they're worth. They're an obstacle course I need to get over. Why the hell am I roaming around at 3 in the morning freezing, wasting my laundry coins on a bunch of selfdeluded assholes?

I walk home, stroll, the night air so pure it singes my lungs, I feel awake for the first time in How long? feel the beginning of relief, feel light, feel like Picasso walking through Paris, loving being conscious while everyone sleeps, feeling more alive by contrast. Why shouldn't I be happy? Maya sold a piece tonight, and not to Dahlia. Somebody bought Wet Dream, loved the waterblue of Phthalo and Viridian, loved my body parts on pedestals. And that platinum guy wants to give me a cybershow and a zine guy was there and Maya said he said good things to her and her press release was fabulous and I was fabulous and my work was.

I think I'll go by the gallery, look in the window, see my name presstyped to the wall. I head down B, see the freaks come out to play, wonder what happened to the Pyramid Club, what happened to the zombies who used to dance on the bar there, wonder when I stopped going out, stopped meeting new people, stopped daring so much. Stopped living up to her.

I look in the window, see my name, see the dark gallery beyond it, my pieces sleeping, the scene at the opening having tired them out. They're so adorable in there all alone, so innocent of what they've done, so pure and beautiful and strong. I love them. I so love them, more than anything else, anyone. They are the truth, I spoke them and I can't take them back. Why should I?

That's me in there. My Kodacolor flesh, no blood, no bones, no urine or decomposing animals. Just my body, a little chopped, a little ennobled by paint and imagination but recognizably human, recognizably me. I can't believe no one said one word about them, not one of my friends could pry themselves apart from Callie long enough to pay the slightest attention to the actual reason we were here tonight. Me. My pieces. I wish I could touch them, touch the plate glass instead, can't believe there's this barrier between those parts of myself and me.

I see my face in the blackness of my name. The pleasing line of jaw and chin, the warble silhouette of hair, the oval eyes, visionary. I am prettier than Callie. Smarter. I can take her. I can beat her at this. I can.

I start with Max. His building's mostly dark, his window, dark. I see it upsidedown, tilt my head back then forward every few minutes, checking. He could be watching me from up there, waiting me out, thinking I'll leave. He's probably not even home, still out with the gang or crashed at Dahlia's.

My legs are asleep. This fucking metal rail has numbed my ass. I'm gonna have a dent if I don't get off it soon. I'm dying to go get a coffee but I hate to leave my perch, hate to miss Max when he struts up the block all untroubled over what he's done to me. He's my only option. I can't do anything with them all together, all glued to each other around Callie. They're probably all at Dahlia's, sitting at Callie's feet, trying to comfort her, trying to make up for me.

I wait, wonder if Max is coming, wonder if Callie's crying her eyes out on his shoulder, wonder if he'll let himself fall for that.

He used to. He used to really ache for Callie, really hurt when she'd cry, really try to understand her, to help her, I saw him. When I showed up, moved in with them, he watched her do it with me, cry to get my pity, to make me think she was defenseless, to disarm me so I'd go to extremes to make her happy. That's when Max knew he'd been wrapped around her too long, too oblivious. He started staying out all night, started getting high, started arguments with her just so she would cry and he could watch without feeling.

One night we met at Tompkins Square Park, the 3 of us. It was cold as hell and we were bundled, on our way to wait in the usual endless movie line, warming our hands on our coffee containers, deflecting the cold, fending off the jangling coffee containers of homeless people, the sprinkling of junkies, skidding on crack vials. Max had a plastic bag with something slimylooking in it. He pulled it out, said Suck don't swallow. Callie made the obvious joke. Max got irritated. The shrooms kicked in. We skipped the movie, wandered around, felt the city, spun the cube at Astor Place for the tourists who were shocked by our kinesis, the cube's, watched it twirl without getting dizzy, got dizzy, went back to their place, had some wine, got sleepy, got complicated. Max started coming on to me, touching me too much, to piss Callie off, to provoke her, to sever her feelings for him. It worked on me instead. I told him to knock it off, quit messing around, quit flirting with me to make Callie jealous. Callie liked my take on it, she tried to believe it. But that backfired, set Max in his resolve, made him leave. For good. He just walked out, left all his stuff. Callie heaved whatever she could out the window. I got the rest. I wish I could've Max. Becky.

He looks surprised. Very. I slide off the numbing rail, want to rub my butt, don't, stand smack in front of him, search his eyes, for anything, throw myself against his chest. Oh Max what am I gonna do? My head's on his shoulder, he can't see my face. I wait to feel his arms hold me. They don't. Max I feel terrible. Sure you do Becky he says acidly. Max please don't be mad at me, I didn't do it on purpose. How could you not have Becky, you're not a stupid woman. I could slap him but I resist. That is not what's called for. I can't bring myself to cry, to test his pity. I can't. I have to try something else.

Where is she Max? He doesn't answer. He just stands there, looking at me, coldly assessing my credibility. Please tell me. He says nothing. Now I'm shivering, I could panic. I watch him, hang on his every movement, see his eyes evade me, feel my desperation go, feel my power over my feelings, feel my voice firm. Max where's Callie. She's at Dahlia's he relents, all snotty. They're all there. Let me come upstairs and call. I think that's a really bad idea Becky, just leave it alone. I start to argue but he goes Don't you know how fragile Callie is? Fragile? He must be kidding. I look at his fist of a face. He's not kidding. Is she ok? Ok? I don't think so Becky. In fact I think you've succeeded where no one else has, she's totally destroyed.

I try to absorb this, his accusations, his validity. I rub my aching head. You really hurt her Becky, and it's hard to believe you didn't do it on purpose. I didn't Max, you saw that piece before anyone and you didn't see her in it. He looks away again. I know it looks bad Max but you don't know how I am when I work. I just get to this place where I'm not thinking anymore, I'm just in it. Haven't you ever had that experience acting? He leans on the rail, he's thinking it over, he's engaged. I've done it.

He looks at me. Are you really suffering over this Becky? Max I say with my smallest voice. It's just that everything comes easy to you Becky, you never seem to struggle for long, you never suffer. I do Max. I watch him teeter. I move into him, put my arms around his soft waist, hold on.

I feel his arms rise slowly, go around my back. We rock a little. Your cheek is frozen Becky. I've been waiting for you for hours. Really? I nod my lie into his scarf, sniff his hair. Becky? Yeah? I'm kind of surprised you came to me. I I I don't say anything else. Come on, let's get you warm. We climb his stoop, still holding on to each other. He feels for his keys in his pocket, pulls them up to the door, drops them, looks at me shyly as he bends to pick them up. I'm in.

His apartment's overheated. I pull off my hat as I turn the deadbolt behind me, I turn from the door, stand face to face with a younger Max, the one on the trash heap, the one who got busted. The pulsing light's flashed his face, a little doll body sticks out of the dirt, the perfect curve of a toilet bowl. I wonder how he managed to get this back from Callie, how he salvaged any of his possessions. He catches me looking at it, smiles at me, tender now, remembering. I actually want to kiss him, not just to get him back.

I'm really hot, drop my scarf to the floor, my coat, pull my sweater over my head, hold it up to him. He takes it, tosses it on his beachchair, I guess that's all he could afford. Is that where I should put the rest Max? He looks at what I'm wearing, sees how little else there is. He pulls off his own sweater, tosses it, messes up his hair, I put it back how it was, he touches mine which is hot on my back. We're still in the hallway. Aren't you gonna invite me in?

He's looking at me, looking alert. His eyes are shiny, surprised. I've provoked an honest reaction from a bad actor. I feel exultant, I feel his cheek which is smooth, my hand slides across it, to the back of his neck, I feel his hair there, smooth. I put my mouth up to his ear, whisper Max, hiss his cheek, kiss it, put my mouth up to his. He is not tentative like Hugh. He is hungry for me, greedy for me, better for me, his tongue tastes like wine. He pushes me up against the wall and my shoulder bumps his picture, my picture. It crashes to the floor. Max goes Forget it, our boots crunch glass, his hands are under my clothes, his hardness pushing against me, releasing me from scheming.

He dances me down the hall. He's got a little gallery of his own, a rogue's gallery, of headshots, of himself, beard here, sideburns there. Max has been living in some bad spy movie, disguising himself from the camera, from his friends, from me.

We fall onto his bed. I try to undress him. He stops

me, turns off his cowboy nightlight, starts to undress me. Max I want to see you. Not yet Becky he begs. It's not his fault. His parents were nudists. I accustom myself to his darkness.

We strip each other, bare, flop around on the covers trying to get our way, his breath is on me, his hands. I put my mouth on him, move him, listen to him wince and breathe, feel him give in to me, feel him harden, feel him moving, shiver, pulse. I get out of the way, feel him shudder, feel him rest. I rest, lay my head on his thigh, mop him up with my hair, feel him straining away from me, hear a click, see the room go bright, see Max, pompous with satisfaction.

He reaches for me. Becky. Come here. I lay my head on his chest, see how pale he is, how taut except around the middle. I've always wondered what you'd be like as a lover. Shh I say. I don't want to talk. I lie on my back, my hair sticky beneath me. I pull him to me, push him down, feel him lick my belly, bite my hipbone, bite my hair with a rush of warm exhaling. That's the kind of lover he is, he knows how to work me. I watch his muscles tense as he does, watch his face. He gives me all his best angles, he gives. He locks on, explores me with his tongue, his fingers. He finds my fingers, pushes them into me, leaves me like that, awkward.

I compose myself, sit up to see where the hell he's going. I'm right here Becky, his voice comes from the window. Another light pops on, on me, blinding me. I shade my eyes. Max is sitting on the sill. I'm sitting on the bed. What's wrong Max? Nothing. I want to watch you. Uh Max I'm not really Wait Becky. He comes back to me, takes my hand again, starts moving it around with his, starts me thinking this could be good. Show me what you like Becky. He lets me go, goes back to the window, props his feet against the frame, wedges himself in. I'm watching him. He's watching me. I flash on my Object of Desire, understand I'm not handless. I get up on my knees, touch myself, feel my thinness, feel my power over Max. His eyes are wet, wide, his hands are folded calmly. Mine are moving surely over me. I feel my nipples aching to be touched and touch them, feel my legs begin to weaken under me, feel how wet I am, feel myself about to go over that edge, fall back, hear Max say Open your legs, yes, that's right. He's watching me. I watch myself, my body moving, willing. I look at Max until I can't.

I hear him clap. The simple crack of applause echoes in his tiny room, in my baffled ears. I hear him rustle toward me, feel the bed give under his weight, I give under it. He wedges himself inside me and I feel a desire after desire, a longing when there's nothing left to want. I start to cry. Max misunderstands, takes my face in his hands. I'm sorry Becky, did I hurt you? He thinks he has that power. But he can't touch me now. None of them can.

ME

After Max winning Dahlia and Hugh will be a cinch. Hugh can be flattered. Dahlia can be guilted. I can do both.

I gulp Max's lousy coffee, burn my tongue, read Max's VOICE, wonder when he'll wake up, when he'll realize what we've done, when he'll feel for me in his bed, when he'll come out here looking for me, to see if I'm still here. I'm here, still, naked, hot remembering. He slept with his nose in my neck, breathed me in while he dreamed, sweetly, endearingly, deceptively. I didn't dream at all.

I need a shower, take one, rinse Max off, my fingers. My scent lingers, no matter how much soap I use. I keep checking, putting my fingers to my nose, obsessively now, weirded out. I never knew he'd done this to Callie, never knew he'd fetishized her, ritualized her, turned other women into her. He must've done it to Dahlia. He must've. She must've been thinking of his applause in the cab on the way to the spa. She hid it well. She's kept quite a few secrets from me. I can't blame her for this one, it's humiliating to be deformed, shaped into a certain someone.

I might be in trouble. I didn't expect this to change my feelings, my plan, my sexual palette, I didn't think it would affect me.

I better go. I don't know what I'm waiting for. I can only lose ground with Max, lose my advantage, lose my head. I write him a note. Gotta go. Love, Becky. I can't trust myself to say more. I can't let a lot of time slip by, Callie will have sucked Dahlia and Hugh back in completely. I can't let that happen, can't let them succumb. They'll be grateful I've rescued them. They'll thank me.

I get my clothes from the hallway, fold Max's hastily, leave them on his beachchair, avoid the glass on the floor by the door. My poor picture lies there, tattered at one edge from the fall. I leave it. I get out, quietly, quickly.

I run down the shabby stinking tenement stairs, out the door, past the rail I inhabited last night in fear, frozen. I am cool again, still calm, determined to recover my friends. To unleash them from Callie.

She must've been up all night, stoking her trauma, suffering for her audience. I can just see her, her poor me expression, her tearblotched face, her delight at having me to exploit, my unconscious, my misstep, at having some new crisis to live for.

How does she have the energy to do this again and again and again? She's been creating disturbances for as long as I can remember, before that. I couldn't sustain the selftorture, wouldn't want to suffer that intensity day after day of my life. I couldn't live that way. I'm beginning to sound like Hugh.

I complete the circle I began last night, this morning, when everything was in doubt. Funny how different my street looks now that I've recovered one thing I'd lost, one friend. Once does not a lover make. Once is what it was. Max will understand that, after everything else I intend has happened. If I can go through with putting the brakes on him. I'm a little shaky on that, floored by images of what we did, by feelings I didn't expect and don't want and have. I loved it. What we did, what I did. There are so many reasons to keep that to myself.

My apartment smells stale, the leftover scent of acrylic. I look at my spasm on the wall, feel its power drain from me, feel mine increase. I open my window, stick my head outside, breathe, look toward the river like that'll make the air I'm inhaling fresher. I can't even see the river. But I know it's there.

Hugh's stuff is still in my bedroom. Good, I can use this, get him to come here. I'll wait for him, let him walk into my hallway, my bedroom, let him think I'm not here, let him gather up his precious possessions, and when he leaves he'll find me huddled, weeping in the corner, suffering, missing him, what we were to each other, what we might've been.

I dial Dahlia. Hello? Dahlia it's Becky. I know she says distastefully. I need to speak to Hugh please. I'll see if he wants to. What a pissy thing to say. She goes away, leaves me dangling. I wait, way longer than I should, way madder than I want to be. I hear nothing in the background, no muffled voices, no crying, no Callie. Footsteps approach. I'm hoping they're Hugh's, please be Hugh's, but I hear icecubes jingling. He won't come to the phone Becky. In a flash I see Dahlia in her apartment, attached to me only by a phone cord. She's so cold, protecting Hugh, protecting herself. From me not Callie. I assemble my anger, it enlightens me. I figured he wouldn't Dahlia. Please tell him I'm going out and he should come get his stuff in the next 2 hours or I can't be responsible for what'll happen to it. All she says is Oh? And tell him to leave my keys on the table. And tell him I never want to see him again. I have worked myself up, am hysterical, am crying as if I believe what I'm saying. And so I hang up on Dahlia.

I've never hung up on Dahlia. I hope that wasn't a mistake, hope I haven't lost maneuverability to emotion, wish I could be sure I know what I'm doing. I can. I can trust my instincts. I can improvise with Hugh. Dahlia will tell him I'm serious. He'll come. He'll be afraid not to.

I grind coffee, let it drip, stake out my apartment, my territory, my Hugh. I can't believe I ever thought I was in love with him. He seemed so cultured at Berkeley, so cosmopolitan with his French music predilection, so deep with his longing for Callie which I mistook for passion. And I wanted that, not some diluted mix of desiring to be desired and familiarity and thereness. Why didn't I notice he was a business major? Why did I never see the sad, base drive for money behind how he makes his living? How can he spend his life propagating culture's commonest expression of insecurity? How could I ever want that?

I don't. I won't. Ever. I know this with all that I am. I know that my life will be more. I will never see Hugh as I did. Maybe I knew all along. And that's why we never were together. Maybe that's why I'm so sad about him now. He's afraid, afraid of life, of me.

He won't come alone. He'll have to bring Dahlia, to protect him. Shit. I hadn't thought of that but now I'm sure The rattle of keys in the door rattles me. I haven't planned what to do. I stand up.

Dahlia walks in. Alone. Always doing other people's dirty work aren't you Dahlia. She just looks at me, disgusted, turns toward my bedroom, goes there, gathers up Hugh's stuff in a rustling hurry. I sit down on my couch, the one I wouldn't have if not for Dahlia. I'm hurt and mad and burning to lash out at her, at them. I listen to her progress, hear the zip of one bag, the other, think, think, what can I do? She rushes up the hall, heads for the door. She's leaving. I could kill her.

Is this how it's gonna end between us Dahl? She hesitates, her shoulders droop, that perfect posture gives way, gives her away. She stands there, slumped unlike herself and I know it's not over, we're not done, she's reasoning with herself, practicing for me. She drops Hugh's bags, turns around. Becky I don't hate you she says deliberately, her hair a mess from rushing. So why are you being like this? I'm afraid of you Becky. I laugh at how earnest she looks. You're afraid of me I say like she's preposterous. She looks at me, dead serious. If you could do that to Callie, intentionally or otherwise, I'm very afraid of what you might do to me.

This had not occurred to me, that I could seriously hurt her. That it would occur to her that I could. I have no reply to this. I can't promise that I would never do such a thing since I'm clearly capable of doing such a thing. My anger escapes me. I'm scared.

Dahlia I love you I blurt out. She stays near the door, not leaving. You're my closest friend in the whole world. I know Becky. I feel that way too. And I know it's inevitable that we hurt the people we love, I just don't know how I can leave myself open to you. You devastated Callie.

I feel so bad in my gut, really terrible, I start to cry. Dahlia's face is struggling, her big heart. Dahlia this whole thing never should have happened. I know Becky, it's partly my fault for wanting to get back at Callie in the first place, I set the whole thing in motion, I realize that, and I've taken responsibility for it. What do you mean? I told Callie it was my idea to invite her to your show so we could punish her with our friendship. It just got out of hand.

I'll say it did I say. I don't say it was the most embarrassing moment of my life, ugly, painful, hurtful and mean, stupid, wrong, futile. Callie's guilt is needsoaked, every hurtful thing she did was unintended to do harm, bears no resemblance to what we did to her, laying a trap, watching her walk into it so we could repair our wounded egos. Besides, we chose her over and over, knowing what she was, difficult, demanding.

Dahlia breaks our silence. Can I just ask you one thing Becky? Yeah, sure, anything. Her face is so open and sweet, her eyes so clear. Did you make that collage for me? I mean to hurt Callie, to avenge me for that night? I'm stunned by the question, made stupid by it. Dahlia waits for me to say something. I don't. I can't. Dahlia thinks this was my own private revenge plan, she thinks I did this intentionally, she has dropped the perfect excuse for my unconscious into my lap. I can't figure out what to say, what will keep her, what will work. I look at my shoes, I fold my arms, I stall as long as I can, hear Dahlia shifting her weight. I look at her, feel tears on my cheeks. I guess I did Dahl, in a way. I was so mad that Callie had abused your generosity, you didn't deserve her rejection. Thank you Becky. She slides down the wall, rests on her haunches. She looks like I feel. Oh Dahlia, I'm sorry I never told you I knew about you and Callie. I just couldn't. It's ok Becky. I should've known better than to try to keep it a secret.

So what do we do now? I ask, wiping my wet face with my palms. I don't know Beck.

We stay all quiet. Finally Dahlia releases herself, sits on my floor. She looks at me, sizes me up. I'm so tired of being looked at like that. Hugh can't stand that you're mad at him, that's why I came instead. I knew he'd melt just walking into your apartment, and here I am doing what he was trying to avoid. He's not mad at me? A thrill of relief shoots through me, suddenly I'm longing to see Hugh. Hugh believes in justice not forgiveness Becky. He thinks Callie deserves whatever she gets. I think he was shocked last night more than anything she says. He's not used to so much excitement. That's true I say. We almost laugh.

I get up again, I go to Dahlia, drop to my knees. I'm so sorry this happened Dahl. Please don't be afraid of me. It's not just you Becky. I'm afraid of everyone.

I hug her, as hard, as gentle as I can. Oh Becky she says, her voice muffled in my hair, why is it so hard to love the people we love? Because we're people? Finally she laughs and I love her so much I could burst.

She pulls herself up from the floor. Can I use your phone Beck? You wouldn't be you if you didn't Dahl. I bring her the phone. She speeddials herself. It's ok Hugh, everything's ok now. She listens to him, says ok, hangs up. He's coming over. What about Callie? She left early this morning. We sat around all night trying to convince her we didn't hate her. She kept asking about you Becky. What about me? She wanted to know if we hated you. Oh. We couldn't say we did. So she left.

I feel a surge of relief and love for my friends, they have forgiven my inadvertent injury, my preoccupation with Callie, my version of their own affliction. They have chosen me, not Callie. I have beaten her at her own game. I cover my face with my hands, feel it for gloating, realize I should show concern, try to make my face comply, say Do you think I should call her or something Dahl? Dahlia's head is tilted like it's weighing what to say. She takes my question with all the sincerity she feels. No. Just let her deal with it. She will. She has to. She knows Max and I are here for her, and she and Hugh at least tolerated each other which is a bit of a breakthrough, as much as they can muster after that much time and resentment. If you want to do the same Beck it's gonna take a lot of work to make up for what you, what happened. Are you ready for that? I shrug but she's insistent. Can you do it Becky? I don't know Dahlia. I really don't know.

My answering machine is frantically blinking. I just left Dahlia and Hugh drinking Vanilla Woodruff at Yaffa, it must be Max. I hesitate to hear his voice, to feel its effect on me, to know who I might become with him. Dahlia managed to stop being his lover et cetera and stay friends. Maybe I can muster that much nerve. I hit Play. Um, hi Becky. It's me. I really need to talk to you. Can you see me this afternoon? Please? Call me as soon as you get this. I really need you.

I call back fast. My heart beats hard and loudly as I dial, reluctant but strangely curious. Hi. Becky? Yeah. Callie's voice cracks, she's crying. Are you ok? No. I really need to see you. Ok, sure, you wanna come here? No. I want you to meet me at the gallery. My gallery? I blurt. Yeah. Why? I want to talk about my collage she says sniffling. Uh oh. Why don't we talk here Callie, I'll make us some NO! I need to see it again and I want you to be with me. Ok. I can be there in like 10 minutes? Me too.

I walk fast downtown, past the sleepy lateopening shops that do not match my pace, my anxiety. I try to figure out what to say. I'm sorry. No. Because I'm not really. Try to forgive me. No, too submissive. I didn't mean to hurt you. Too concessionary, and I can't vouch for my unconscious.

I arrive in 15. I say hi to the parttime gallery girl with the tonguestud and pierced eyebrow. She has no idea who I am, continues her speechimpedimented phone conversation without raising an earring. I'm thinking I'll have to rat on her to Maya. I interrupt. Is Maya in? She's at lunch Galgirl says thickly, without moving the phone from her face, basically ignoring me. I decide to be generous. It's not her fault I'm on edge.

I don't see Callie. I check my watch, feel relieved she's later than me, walk around the gallery, feel bad about my pieces, look at them hard, wonder what they are, what else I might have divulged in them, who else I might have injured. I look at Lips Stick. Did I hurt Dahlia by making it? No, she saw it as I intended, as a sympathetic portrait, a portrait of abuse, abuse of power, of trust, of family, of a body helpless and whole. Is it because I had her consent, her participation in the making that makes this different from my portrait of Callie? Is it my unconsciousness that wounds Callie most? Would she prefer that I'd done it on purpose? Does she think I did? I look at each collage in turn, look but don't see anything but what I made, art in a particular history, not only my own, it merges me and paint and photographic images and canvas and precedent, not attack and confession and disloyalty to the only people who love me.

I round the corner to Monumental Vanity. It's Callie. She's bundled in chocolate fake fur, hands stuffed in her fuzzy pockets. Her eyes blink slow. She looks drunk. I'm in trouble.

It's actually quite beautiful Becky. She acts like the conversation's already started. She acts like she knows the collage by heart. She's not looking at it as she says I really like the texture you created Becky, the way you made the candles twinkle with just a few blobs of gold paint. I'm impressed. You really perfected your technique, you made a genuine work of art out of my painfully obvious defects.

She really does look quite fragile and I'm pinched by my lack of concern which is mutating as I watch her coming to terms with my view of her. Oh Callie I'm so sorry it came out like this, I didn't realize what I But you know Becky, it's kind of like when we were in college, you always had a really lousy sense of color. What? She moves up close to the canvas, looks at the paint, sways a little. I try to hold her by her furred arm. She backs away from me, afraid of me, unsteady.

Her eyes flicker heavily, I want to gouge my fingers into them, keep her from blinking, I want to make her look at the image, I want to make her see. Look Callie, don't you see that this is me? I didn't realize what I was doing when I made it but look closely, please, look deeper, I was taking your pain on myself. Don't you see that? Don't you see No I don't see that Becky. I see that you've ridiculed me about a really low point in my life and that you've exposed my biggest failings as a human being and that you must truly hate me and that I must be that unlovable. Callie I And you obviously need my help with your biggest failing as an artist. Do we really have to do this Callie? Don't you appreciate my art criticism? Don't you see that what your precious collage needs is a splash of color?

I'm not looking at the piece, I'm looking at her, her eyes, as big as they'll get with her anger, her mouth with its horrible indictments spewing out, her body stuffed into her coat like a straightjacket. But she's in motion, she flings herself at the collage, she draws her hands out of her pockets, rubs herself on the canvas, streaking it crimson. Callie my god what are you doing? She pulls herself back, staggers. Her sleeves splatter blood, stain the stark white gallery floor. Don't you see that's so much better Becky? She's getting fuzzier. You see Becky? you detest me but I help you. That's what friends are for, don't you see? I see the blood, feel the familiar white noise rush into my head, a humming shuts out all sounds, my visual field chokes, I feel the hot pressure of my body defending me from memory, from the fear that I can taste in my mouth. I want to vomit, can't get any air into my tightening lungs, feel my legs giving way beneath me. All I can force from my throat is NO.

I hear fluttering. It must be my heart.

Maya is standing over me waving a press release about me in my face. Oh finally she's coming to. Callie. Is that her name? Where is she I demand. I sit up, too fast, my head aches, I'm clammy, wet along one side of my body with Callie's blood. I can't look at it, at it on me.

Where's Callie? She's gone Maya reports, all unconcerned. Is she ok? I have no idea, she left before I got back. We have to find her Maya. Hurry. Help me up?

Maya conveys me to the phone. I dial Dahlia. Hello? Dahlia get over to Callie's as soon as Becky she's not there. Dahlia's voice is low, grave. Where is she Dahlia? I don't know! she left me a note saying she'd be dead by the time I found it, I called the police and they went right to her place and she wasn't there so we rode around in the patrol car looking for her but she's nowhere I could think to look. Did you try Max? Of course I tried Max, I tried everyone Becky. She was here Dahlia, like 20 minutes ago? I say looking at my watch, then Galgirl nods, watching me curiously. Dahlia's voice rises, surprised, suspicious. She went to your place? No I'm at the gallery. What? She she She what Becky? Becky? She cut herself Dahl, I think she slit her wrists. Oh no, no no no no Dahlia will be hysterical soon. Her escalating fear urges my own. Dahlia listen to me. Did you check the emergency rooms? Yeah but she wasn't there. What happened Becky? Call the police back Dahl, tell them to try the hospitals again. Becky what happened? And the streets near the gallery. I'm thinking And the morgue but I don't say that. Dahlia will think of it herself. I hang up, scratch Dahlia's number onto a pad for Maya, just in case. I follow the trail of blooddrops out the gallery door, down the steps to the grungy sidewalk, toward the east, toward the river. Blood on concrete doesn't make me so woozy, it gets absorbed, into the pavement, into the muck of what other people've left behind, it looks normal. I move fast, feel bewildered, my eyes trained on the spots that lead me away from the gallery, the blots that Callie made as she ran from me, the force and violence of her in evidence beneath my feet. I keep looking, scan doorways and shopwindows, slam into a couple linked by their arms, I crush their shopping bags, avoid looking into their faces, avoid thinking, focus, focus. A couple of drops more and the spatters disappear. There is no trace left of Callie.

When I get to Dahlia's I hit her intercom so hard my hand stings. Her tinny voice says Callie? No it's me. There's a pause, too long, and then the door releases, letting me into the small dark hallway to the elevator. I press Dahlia's floor and ride the same ride I did when everything was good. I'm afraid. Callie can't be dead if Dahlia thought I was her. Maybe she called. Maybe she's on her way here now, wrists cleaned and bandaged.

Maybe she just jumped in a cab and got to an ER and now wants to come see us suffering over her. I can't stop seeing her in the pristine gallery, spattering the floor, the walls, my collage. Just imagining all the blood makes me hot, dizzy. I can't look at myself, my clothes all stained with Callie. I suck in the elevator air, stale and disappointed, wish the ancient thing would go faster and get me there. It finally stops with a bounce and a hum as the door slides open to Dahlia's open door. Hugh's standing there waiting, for me.

You ok Becky? Yeah, you know, just worried, have you heard anything? The police haven't called in an hour he says as he takes my coat off me, distractedly carries it into the livingroom. Where's Dahlia? She's taking a bath. She's so stressed out she said she was going to strain something if she didn't relax. I leave Hugh in the livingroom holding my bloody coat and walk to the bathroom and Dahlia. The door's ajar, a heatlamp burns steam and forces golden light into a slice of the hall. I say as calmly as I can Dahl? I hear water startle, then Dahlia's voice. Becky? Yeah I say as I push into the heavy room. Through the mist I see the footed castiron tub, Dahlia's arm draped over one side, the rest of her invisible. She comes up for air batting suds and water from her eyes and sputtering mouth. Becky. What happened? I sit in a leopardskin chair next to the tub and watch Dahlia cross her arms on the tub's rim and drop her lovely chin on top of them. She is looking up at me like I have an answer.

I put my hand on her wet head and say She called and wanted me to meet her at the gallery. What time? she demands. Uh, it must have been about 11:30 when she called. When did you find her note? When Hugh and I got back from Yaffa. It was stuck in the window grate of the frontdoor. I almost didn't see it, it was just a scrap of paper with my name scribbled lightly on it. Oh god Dahlia. I can't believe Callie would do this. You didn't see her last night Becky. It was like she'd been waiting for some chance for forgiveness from us and we just slammed her face in it. You mean me, you mean I did. No, I already told you I know I started this. She looks at the phone standing out of place on the sink. Why don't they call? What did they say they're doing Dahl? They're just out looking for her near the gallery and any place we told them she might be likely to go. Did you try Max? Yeah but he's working and his machine broke and Hey you guys? Hugh almost whispers, softly tapping on the door, I can't take being alone out here. Oh just come in Hugh Dahlia says, irritated. He tries to avert his eyes from Dahlia who's still in her tub, he sits angled away from her on the floor. So Becky, what happened? he wants to know, is that what I think it is all over your coat?

I nod, start over. She wanted to meet me at the gallery but when I got there she was all dopey and strange and saying I'd exposed her at her worst to the world and then she threw herself on that fucking collage and she was bleeding like anything, she'd had her hands in her pockets the whole time. Shit, you passed out, didn't you? Hugh says, exasperated with me. I nod. And she ran out of there while I was out and when I came to I followed the blood out the door but it started disappearing like a block away, she must've put her hands back in her pockets or jumped into a cab. Dahlia's eyes are stuck on me. Did you tell the police this Becky? No, I thought you called them Dahl. I did call them, don't be dense! I feel myself blushing. Tears sting my eyes. I've never seen Dahlia be cruel to anyone. She's sitting straight up now and Hugh forgets to look away. Obviously you need to tell them that Becky. Now Dahlia stands, regal in her tub and snarling at Hugh Give me that towel Hugh. Becky, take the phone and dial the number on the diningtable for the precinct. Hugh, go show her where it is. Hugh and I get up to carry out Dahlia's commands. As soon as I grasp the phone it rings and we all freeze. Hello? I say more urgently curious than I've ever been in my life to know who's calling. Max's voice says Dahlia. No Max it's Becky, have you heard from What the fuck is going on? I got this insane note from Callie. You did too? Dahlia and Hugh stare at my mouth, sort my every word. Dahlia's let her towel dip into the tub. Hugh goes Shouldn't you get off the phone in case someone's trying to call? Dahlia barks I have call waiting! Max goes Is she nuts? Max what does it say? I hear the rustling of paper then Max saying It says Goodbye Max. I never stopped loving you. Don't forget that, no matter what happens. What the fuck is she trying to pull? Max this is serious I say. Dahlia tromps out of the tub and grabs the phone and says What did yours say Max? She listens closely then says gently Why don't you come over now. We'll explain everything when you get here. Ok. See you soon. She shuts off the phone and says I thought it would be better not to tell him what's happening over the phone. Like we didn't gather. Let me get dressed you guys. Why don't you make us a drink. I want a scotch in the tallest glass I have. You know where it is Becky. But call the police and tell them what you know. Do that first. She's in some high alert mode ordering us around. This scares me more than anything.

I hurry to the diningroom, punch the number to the precinct, ask for Sergeant Sanders, tell him the story. He listens, then he says Now why would she do this? Uh. Well. I uh. I am trying to figure out a way to say. He supplies me with an answer. Has she always been unstable? Yes I say, she's an unstable person. Hugh glares at me. But I never thought she'd I stop, unable to blame Callie for what's happening. I don't tell Sergeant Sanders it's all my fault, but Hugh knows it, his glassy eyes like marbles hard and round and capable of shooting mine out of their sockets. Ok Miss, I'll radio this info to the squad car but they already knew to check near that art gallery. I wish Dahlia could've heard that, she would have to take back her idiotic insult. And you'll let us know as soon as you find her Sergeant? Will do Miss, I have the number, the other young lady left it several times. Thank you Sergeant. Sure thing.

Hugh is watching me. Has he ever done anything but? What? I whine. She's an unstable person? he's gonna have those cops looking for a nutcase. Well who else would pull such a thing Hugh? I can't help it, I'm sick of being attacked but Hugh isn't going to let up, he comes toward me, his arms bent, his hands clutching air. I don't even recognize you anymore Becky, you've gotten so hard. At least one of us can rolls off my tongue like it's been sitting on the tip of it. I see the shock spread over Hugh's face and wish I could take it back. Hugh I didn't mean it. Fuck off Becky.

He turns away from me, starts rummaging in the cupboards, starts ransacking them, starts banging the doors shut. All the glasses shudder, the thick ceramic plates. What are you doing Hugh? Looking for the goddamned scotch. I almost laugh, his anger is such a relief. It's in the hall closet in a wicker basket, Dahlia hides it from the cleaning lady. I'll get it I say. I'll get it he grunts and stomps out of the kitchen.

Fuck him. My head is killing me. I need a coffee. No way Dahlia has any. Maybe Life delivers. It's right on the corner, I'll get my fix fast. I call information, dial Life Cafe, order some stuff with the coffee just to make the minimum. Max'll eat it.

I fall down on the couch, wait for the coffee to come, for Max. I was distracted when we spoke just now, but I wonder how I'll feel seeing him. I look out the window at the tops of the trees that spring out of Tompkins Square. They sway serenely and calm my nerves. Hugh stomps back to the kitchen, ignoring me, my peacefulness. He hates my guts. I wonder if I'll ever see him again, after all that's happened between us. I wonder if I'll miss him. If I'll miss Callie. Oh my god. I must think she's dead. What if she is dead? No one else is saying it, I'm not gonna be the one to say it out loud. I can't risk being unforgiven for one more thing. Dahlia would never see me again. I've already confirmed all her worst fears about being close. Max would cut me off too. What pleasure could we give each other after causing something like that? Any of us? We couldn't stand to look at each other, our guilt would be too palpably gruesome, that's all we would reflect at each other. Shit. She can't be dead. There's no revenge as complete as suicide. Oh god what if she's dead. What have I done? How could I not have recognized real pain? Why couldn't I separate Callie's aching, gnawing injury from its repetitive expression. She was just so relentless. I didn't know there could be a threshold you could cross beyond which endurance isn't possible. I pushed Callie over hers. That's psychological autopsy, not excuse. There's no excuse for what I've done. No excuse. I feel all flushed. My body's humming. I pace, walk off some dread, hear Hugh fixing Dahlia her large scotch.

The delivery guy arrives with the sweetpotato fries and coffee. I give him a huge tip, his puzzled face tells me he thinks I made a mistake. I watch him struggle with his conscience. It's a short battle, he stuffs the bills in his pocket and takes off. Max appears at the top of the stairs. Hi he says softly. Hi. I look at his mouth as he comes in the door. I kiss his cheek. What the fuck's going on? He runs his hand down my sleeve. I take his hand, pull him into the livingroom. I try to give him the short version of the scene at the gallery. It's looking like Callie slit her wrists and wandered off somewhere. Dahlia's come in, hears me. Very compassionate Becky. Oh excuse me Miss Get Me a Scotch, that's a much more humane response. What is wrong with the two of you? Max growls. Dahlia says Look Max we're waiting to hear if she's dead or alive ok? that's what's wrong with us.

I look at Max and say She's just giving us a good scare. She's probably just pulling a stunt, it might not even have been real blood, it's probably Halloween blood or food coloring. Hugh's back, he hands Dahlia her drink, says snottily So Becky your exquisite sensitivity can't tell real blood from vampire blood? What's that supposed to mean? Max jumps in, defending me even though he doesn't have a clue what Hugh's talking about. I fainted Max. You did? Yeah. I'm not good at blood. Dahlia spits an icecube into her scotch glass and says Maybe we should get the police to analyze it. I'm gonna call them. She goes to find the phone. Do you want the precinct number Dahl? I yell after her. I have redial! she snaps.

Max goes Ok, from the top Becky. You got a note? No I got a call. So you're the only one she called. Right I nod. Didn't you think it was strange that she wanted to meet at the gallery? Yeah but she was crying, it was just like the old days. Ok, so what hap Dahlia comes into the livingroom. Her hand's gripping the phone. She's very still. I feel my stomach drop. Dahlia? Her head starts to move up and down, she's nodding her head. They found her. They've found Callie.

We smash ourselves into a cab, speed down B to get to Callie. Open the window Max? Sure Becky. Not so much! Hugh whines, his hair's getting all displaced in the windstream. Dahlia goes Oh for god's sake Hugh who cares how your hair looks at the moment. Hugh looks at her with his mouth stuck open, like he's suffered some huge injustice he can't wrap his lips around. Dahlia's totally unconcerned, sitting forward on the seat between Hugh and me, breathing down the driver's neck like that will make him go faster. We're already flying, and we're only going a few blocks. We should've just run. I can see us all hurtling on foot past Tompkins Square Park like we're in some romping Beatles movie, Help! while Callie lies waiting, thinking When will they get here?

hurry, hurry. If she's even conscious. I have no idea what to expect beyond She's not dead, the doctors have her under observation. That's all Dahlia told us. That's all she knows. I feel strangely empty, strangely normal in a Callie crisis. It's my friends who are not normal at all. Max, way up front with the driver, his profile all scrunched, keeps touching his face with his fingertips, like a pointillist with 5 blunt brushes dabbing at warped canvas. Dahlia's still pressed forward, her posture's a mess, all misaligned and taking the potholes badly. Hugh's still trying to ward off the wind with his hands which are cupped and bony and red. No one's said anything really since we left Dahlia's. We have nothing left to say to each other.

On the right! Dahlia grunts and we pull over in front of the hospital. Dahlia foists some singles at the driver with one hand and with the other pushes Hugh saying Get out. The taxi zooms away, Dahlia leads us into the revolving door, past the cheesy giftshop, up a marble step to the reception desk. She's on 5 the receptionist says, but you can't all go in at once. We walk to the elevator. Dahlia presses the up arrow about 20 times. Max goes I'll meet you there, looks around for the stairs. I'm going with you I say grabbing his arm. Yeah me too Dahlia says. Hugh follows us, the sheep.

We start the hike up. Dahlia blows past me, taking 2 steps at a time with that stride that's never come in so handy. Each stair creaks, the narrow staircase groans with our progress. Hugh is behind me, breathing heavy. I keep glancing over my shoulder at him but he won't look at me. He looks appalled by his surroundings. I see him reach into his pocket, he pulls out a hankie like the banister might contage him. Max is a few steps ahead of me. I watch his legs work the stairs. I know it's a byproduct of his claustrophobia but he actually looks athletic from this angle.

I reach the landing on 4 and on 5 above me I hear Dahlia's echoing voice saying I'm her friend. I'm wondering how she can possibly characterize herself that way, but I guess she has to say something. I hear a man say I'm Doctor Berkman, all official. I notice my heart's pumping hard, I look up at Max who's looking down at me, I run around him on the skinny landing, rush up the stairs, push through the door into a long corridor, horribly lit, smelly like sour bedsheets.

I start to sweat a little, don't slow down, can't. I have every reason to move in the opposite direction, after all I'm going where I'm not wanted. But I don't turn and run, don't slow down, don't stop doing what I'm doing.

How can I. Everyone I love is headed where I'm headed. Because of me.

I get to Callie's room, feel a slam deep down inside me, a fear, a no, know I shouldn't go in, don't want to know what's going on inside. I plant myself outside, where I belong. The hospital's quiet, the only sounds are rushhour cars rushing down 7th, the clink of bottles and cans as a gloved janitor sorts the trash in the metal basket near the elevator. I wonder when I'll stop sweating. I wait for Dahlia to come out, wish my legs wouldn't shake, lean against the wall, try to steady myself, notice how stretched my sweater is from clutching it around me.

The door swings open. I hide behind it, can't let Callie see me, can't wound her with my presence, can't be attacked with her anguish. It's someone medical coming out, the doctor, white coat crisp, efficient. Are you a relative? he asks. No, just a friend. He nods, moves on quickly to the next victim of disease or accident or bad intentions. I don't stop him, I'm afraid to ask him anything, afraid.

Max arrives behind me, then Hugh, panting. Aren't you going in Becky? Max asks. Nope, you guys go ahead, I'm gonna wait. Hugh goes Only 2 of us can go in at a time and I want to be there for Dahlia. Fine Max says, I need a cigarette anyway. Since when do you I'll be right back Becky he says rushing back down the stairs. Hugh's knocking on the door, listening at it, he pauses when no sound comes back, raises his fist to knock again, hesitates, looks in the little window, waves, nods, finally goes in.

I can't not look, I peer in, discreetly, see Callie lying there, see the giant bottles hanging over her, the clear liquid that must be dripping into her veins, notice 2 uniformed officers, the man cop standing near the fire escape window like in case someone gets the urge to jump, the woman cop sitting on the empty bed near Callie's. Dahlia's standing at Callie's feet, just standing there, just looking at Callie, like she's willing her to move, to wake up, to be ok. Hugh's keeping his distance from Callie, he's hovering near Dahlia, zipping and unzipping his coat.

Max comes back with a lit cigarette, holds it up like a prize, goes You can always count on the psycho ward waiting room. He looks up and down the hall to see if anyone will stop him from smoking it. I go Maybe you should find someplace a little less conspicuous. He nods, distracted, too tense to even give me a look, to give me anything resembling intimacy. What do I expect? he's still Max after all, how could I forget that?

Dahlia walks out. She's moving slowly, purposefully, her long legs taking baby steps. She's standing near the door, looking for Max who's smoking melodramatically a few doors down, scanning the corridor, playing another scene in his imaginary movie. Hugh walks out, he looks flustered, he looks past me, superfluous Hugh, he goes to Dahlia, troubled Max steps on his cigarette and comes to her, magnetic Dahlia, the positive attracting all the negativity around her. I stay where I am. Dahlia moves toward me slightly as my name leaves her body. What did the doctor say? is she ok? I manage. She's dandy Hugh snipes. Max rolls his eyes at Hugh, Dahlia goes she's tranquilized Becky. Should I go in? You don't have to you know Dahlia says impatiently, only do it if you really want to. I look at them, on the verge of knowing what I want, wishing I could have a couple of minutes to myself, to figure out what I should do, what would be best for Callie right now, for me.

I go in, hoping they won't follow. Just the cops and me thinking through Callie, that's what I want. Max whispers Fuck the rules, they all follow me in, they won't leave me alone with Callie, they're afraid we'll make up, afraid we'll get along without them. Callie lies there, her wrists crossed, bandaged. Her eyes are closed, she looks harmless, sweet again, I have the urge to kiss her like a prince.

Dahlia and the man cop are whispering to each other. Hugh says What's going on? to no one in particular. I shrug, Max shakes his head and points at Dahlia like she's in charge of getting us the facts. We're all a little unnerved by police involvement, something new in Callie's repertoire. It's weird to have strangers be part of it isn't it Max? I whisper. He frowns and nods, he's a mess, he needs a shave. Dahlia's nodding too, officially at the cop. In 4 steps she's with us again, pushing us back out the door.

In the hollow space of the hospital corridor Dahlia goes I could kill her. Her voice is low, serious. What happened? Max says. The cops found her, you won't believe this, sitting in Life Cafe watching my building from the window. They were on their way over to pick up all the notes she left us and they spotted someone who matched Callie's description calmly drinking a coffee. She was watching us! Dahlia's livid, her anger ricochets around the corridor. She's starting to pace. Callie set us all in motion, just to see what we would do. Hugh goes So the blood was fake? and gives me a little gloaty glance.

No, she really sliced at her wrists but just enough to make them bleed, it was never life threatening at all. So why is she in a hospital bed unconscious with cops guarding her? Max wants to know. Well she was pretty drunk they said, and they thought she might really be suicidal so they didn't want to leave her alone and there was no family they could find to call. So we're supposed to The door opens, the cops have gathered themselves up to leave. The woman cop walks out first, her big radio and nightstick widening her hips in a way that almost makes her have to turn sideways to get through the door. See that your friend gets some help she says pushing past us. The man cop stays inside holding the door open for us, he won't leave until we look like we're staying. I should get out of here now, I should get out while I can, walking back in there is some kind of promise I don't think I can make. The cop goes Well? I look at his stern, caring face. I don't have the guts to disobey him, his silent command. We all file past him, closing the door, sealing ourselves in.

We just stand there, looking at Callie who's still out, laid out. I'm glad she's not dead I whisper stupidly. Everyone just looks at me. I'm not sure who agrees with me at this point. Max goes I know you're relieved Becky but don't you fucking want to slap her? I do but look at her. They do. Her little mouth's open a little, her hair's a silken pillow for that thick skull of hers. And by the time she wakes up I'll probably just be so sick and tired of all this I will've lost the urge to slap her. Max nods, goes Do you think she's really suicidal? He sounds really gossipy. Dahlia and Hugh are both shaking their heads emphatically. Dahlia goes No way. Just a stunt. Hugh adds In a long line of stunts.

They seem so resolute about her, I feel sorry for her, all alone, all extreme, all hospitalized and helpless. She's gonna be sick you know I say, almost feeling how queasy she'll be when she comes to, how twingey and tender her wrists will be. Dahlia goes Oh no, I'll stay until she wakes up, I'm gonna make her call her mother, but that's it, I'm outta here, I'm not holding her hand while she vomits. Maybe she'll choke on it Hugh says. Max says That's a little harsh isn't it Hugh? If I want the opinion of a total loser Max I'll ask a bag lady. Shut up Dahlia moans.

I watch them totally lose it. I'm pleasantly detached from their bickering, watching Callie sleep through it, wondering if she's registering their upsetness on some level, wondering if it pleases her. Why wouldn't it? It's about her isn't it? Or is it? At least Callie has an excuse for all her senseless effort. She has no art to turn to.

Maybe she's moving toward something, but right now we're her canvas, she's still painting on us. More like welding us together. The way I see it, we owe Callie right now, there's no reason to be miserable about it. What I can't figure out is whether my friends just need to be miserable. They've supposedly found their thing in life and still they fuck it up, their work, their relationships. Dahlia lives in her tower, Max in his spy movie, Hugh in his corporate mould. At least Callie's still longing.

Max says Think we could smuggle in some takeout? There's this great Indian joint near here. Callie and I used to order in from there in summer, it was so hot we'd drag our futon up the fire escape to the roof and lay under the stars eating curry and making love. I imagine the neighbors hearing their moans and gasps from the rooftop. Then the surprising sound of applause. As long as we've all known each other, as long as we've been friends, our common language has always been Callie past tense. I'm beginning to think it always will be.

I hear her start to shift in her sheet. I get a plastic kidney looking pan from the tray on wheels, take it to her, put her hands on the rim so she knows it's there, make sure she can hold it even if she can't open her eyes yet. I go to the bathroom for a papertowel, run cold water over it, take it back to her, drape it over her forehead.

Thank you she mutters, starting to come to. The others crowd around the bed, watch her try to shake off her grogginess.

I take her hand, soft in its limp flatness. Do not touch me she says, low and threatening. I look at her eyes which have popped open, glaring, registering me. I let go of her. Tears start to burn behind my eyes, surprising, choking my voice. Callie. Leave me alone now Becky, I mean it. Callie looks savage, at me, says After everything that's happened what do you really think we can be to each other? She has spit my words at me, the ones I used to push her away. And she's right. I was right. I just have to get used to the idea again, I just have to be strong enough to hold on to that truth. But I can't even stop myself from crying.

I taste the salt of tears and makeup. Callie turns her head away from me. Dahlia brushes Callie's hair from her face, impatience and pity mixing on Dahlia's. Max goes Shh, save your strength Callie. I watch them through my swelling eyes, my face raw as I wipe it dry for a better view of them clustering around her, seeing to her needs, stroking her, comforting her.

My tears stop, freeze, harden. I'm so tired. How many times have I looked at this tableau? How many times will I? Callie's eyes flicker, she's losing steam, she's going under again, or pretending to now that her reflex for drama has kicked in, now that she's given me my cue. The room is quiet. Everyone is staying totally still. We all know what's supposed to happen now. I'm supposed to keep crying, say Please, how can you blame me? Say How can you punish me for what happened? Then Hugh's supposed to say Get over yourself Becky, you're not the scapegoat you imagine, none of us is innocent. Then Max will defend me, say You're such an idiot Hugh. You're such a fuckup Hugh will say back to him. Then I should say I can't believe I've put up with all of you as long as I have. Hugh you're a total coward. Max my darling you are a fuckup and a very sick one. And Dahlia, you are a victim par excellence, and I really think you always will be. But I know that if I keep crying, if I say what I really feel about my friends, this will never end. We will keep doing what we always do, we will keep distracting ourselves with Callie, never facing ourselves, our emptiness, never replacing it with anything real or sustaining.

I should shout at them, I want to. But I don't. I won't. Because I see it now, I see what I should've seen a long time ago. I'm not over it. I'm beyond it. Sick to death of it. I stay out of it, let it go, Callie's provocation, her crisis, this diversion of a life my friends won't let go of.

Callie's breathing deepens. Dahlia goes to sit down on the unoccupied bed. Hugh joins her, their legs dangle. Max takes a fake leather armchair, pats his legs like I should go sit on him. Like that would be comforting. I'm just standing by the door, unable to say or feel anything they'll understand. I raise my hand to wave at them, see their stunned faces as they watch my progress, see their unbelieving eyes as they watch me walk out on them.

I'm suspended in thick red air. I'm trying to get to something but I can't. I feel my heart tingling like I'm going to panic. I force myself, push myself through the crimson atmosphere, dense, looking for something to grab on to, to pull myself through. I wish I could fly instead of pushing like I am. I panic, feel the noise in my head like pressure, like ringing.

I turn off my alarm, look around my room, shake off my dream hangover, wish someone would bring me coffee. There is no one.

I get my own coffee, don't enjoy it, don't feel warmed or revived, don't feel anything but the gnawing promise of more panic, get myself dressed without looking in the mirror. I have to go to work like a good girl.

I head down A, hug my sweater to me as I walk. It's

not cold but I'm shivering. I shuffle into the overdesigned lobby. The frontdesk guy greets me grimly, pushes the elevator button for me like I'm incompetent with everything, not just people. My slow ascent is excruciating, lonely. I have taken this ride for years and not noticed how hard it is to breathe in the tiny little space of the elevator. I'm beginning to feel like I'll never have more room to move in than this, no fresh air, no one to talk to.

The doors release me on 9, I hurl myself into the airy loft, wave mutely at the receptionist. She looks at me, looks through me, does not acknowledge my existence.

My desk is covered with While You Were Outs. My voicemail must be full. I glance at the hasty, resentful scrawl of the receptionist. Not one workrelated request. I fall into my chair, roll backwards a bit, grab the edge of my desk, pull myself up to it. I flick on my lighttable. I pick up a transparency. Little people crawl around the Garden of Delights, naked, playful, innocent. I wonder what Bosch was conscious of when he first began to sketch, to paint. Was he a sexual libertarian or a satirist of sin and aberration or was he working through some preFreudian trauma he wasn't even aware of? I examine the whole triptych, each panel, the details the photographer thought someone would want to reproduce. The sinewy, diabolic tree, the giant pair of ears joined by a redfeathered arrow and phallically sporting a knifeblade, the aortic dwelling being entered by a hooded man with an arrow in his anus as he climbs into The phone rings. I ignore it, hope someone will answer my line for me. I try to remember why I have this pile of images on my desk, what I'm supposed to illustrate. I wonder what photo editor request I'd match to the image I keep seeing when I close my eyes. What was I working on yesterday? The phone rings.

I look around, Terri looks away when I try to catch her eye, I see the gawking faces of the other photo researchers. Everyone watches me, to see what I'll perpetrate next, to see if my cruelty shows. My coworkers know what happened, everyone knows thanks to Maya, the whole stupid mess was on NY1, replayed every halfhour on Headline News. Artist Provokes Suicide Attempt. I clear my voicemail of painful questions, reminders, nosy speculation, obscenities. I do not write down names, phone numbers, email addresses, news channels, station call numbers. I resent the ugly access to fame I've been given.

My phone rings, I watch it, let my voicemail pick up. I can't stand the prying, the smarmy publicity. I can't take calls at The Archive anymore. I can't do my job anymore. I put down my loupe. I go to my boss. I close his door. I quit. No questions asked. Eli looks relieved. He doesn't offer a leave of absence. He won't miss me. There's no one to miss me now.

I walk out to Lafayette, east toward home. I take off my sweater, tie up my waist with it, tie up my hair so my neck can feel the sweet warm breeze. Strange that I ever felt at home in the East Village, it smells sour and the attractive people are unkempt. This neighborhood is so over. Maybe I'll move to Chelsea.

I wait for the light at St Mark's and 2nd. A guy hands me a flyer for body piercing. Illustrated. I cross the street. A heavily pierced woman hands me her flyer. Hades Pain Salon. FREE sample amputation with this flyer. This has always been a neighborhood for extremists, a place you could get away with anything. Fuck Chelsea, this is where I belong.

I think I'll go to the park, I haven't actually been in it forever. I walk with purpose now, join the dregs of humanity that trickle into Tompkins Square, when did the drug dealers let the old people back? I catch my reflection in a window, wonder why I don't look different. Maybe I should pierce something. I've already done the amputation.

I'm tempted to stop for a coffee, sit outside in a nice cafe, test my new notoriousness, see if anyone will recognize me. But, like always, when I go someplace new, alone, I feel a surge of fear. That I cannot overcome.

My building's quiet and I want to scream. I want someone to hear me. I check my mail, see the fancy invitation envelopes and postcards beautifully outnumber the junkmail, wish I could comply with the AND GUEST exhortations.

My frontdoor squeaks a cartoon laugh at me. I drop my bag on the floor, drop my sweater, my invulnerable attitude. Relieved, at home, not under scrutiny. I walk to the window, look out, see nothing at all of interest, walk back to the hall, think I'll pick up my sweater, step over it, fling myself on my bed, lie there for 2 seconds, exhausted, can't stay still, wrench myself up, go to the kitchen, make coffee. The light in my apartment really sucks this time of day. I never noticed that before.

I sit down at my table, enlarged, in vain, sip my coffee, cup 6. I look around my apartment, see the blob still there, the black mark on my wall. I haven't picked up a brush since my show, unable to smell paint or glue, to kindle my unconscious. I have been stripped of my refuge, my pleasure, my work. Naked I. My coffee tastes funny, the half and half has gone bad since this morning or maybe I just didn't notice. I drink it anyway.

I force myself from my stupor, go to my cupboard,

empty of paint, take out the biggest brush I can find. I still have gesso. That will do. I open the bottle, squeeze the milky primer onto my brush, consider eating it. Don't. Death by gesso would be ridiculous. I stroke smoothly across the blackness, white it out, prime my wall, gently. I stop, wait, blow, wait, reapply, blot out the mess I made almost completely. It's good like this.

I look around, at all my empty walls. Hugh would like it like this. But Hugh will never see it. Hugh is long gone. The friends who have loved me for years, no matter what, all gone.

And yet. Callie has saved me from becoming her, and not just with Max. But when she put the razor to her skin, when she hatched her plan to violate my work, to make it unalterably hers, to take from me what I loved most, when she called me to beg me to meet her, she knew, she knew that she had me, that I would succumb to my weakness, she knew my most painful wounds and she used that knowledge against me. Still, she was responsible for flinging me into the spotlight, for giving me the allure of someone worth wanting to die over. But I will always question the interest in me. I will always doubt myself as I never did before. I will never work again as I did, I will never be able to separate my triumphs from her. The Callie collage, her exquisite corpse, the still life I turned her into, sold for an obscene amount of money. Even the other works sold, sold by association with my failure as a friend. Maybe that means Callie won. Maybe.

I flop on my couch, sniff it like it should smell like Dahlia, like her sheets I was between just days ago. I hold the gessoed paintbrush in the air, close my eyes, wait for an image to appear in the blackness of my brain, see only red, liquid and dark and overflowing whatever my mind constructs to contain it.

My Callie collage, the only one with a frame, a mirror that contained her in a way I never could, it gave her what she never could quite muster from us, from me, someone to love her. Now I know, after all the coverage and dissection, she will exist as long as paint and glue and blood.

And that is more than I can say for Dahlia, or Max or Hugh. They have disappeared already.

I'll get over it. I have new furniture to keep me company. I have a new studio space. I have a new show to prepare for. No more dismemberment. No more reassembling. Just paint.

ACKNOWLEDGMENTS

I am utter gratitude for Dani Shapiro, gifted teacher, gift. For their critical contributions to drafts of this book and for other generous acts, I thank Dani, Claire Messud, Margot Livesey, Laura Catherine Brown, Alice Elman, Ariel Leve, Susie Rutherford, Ellen Schutz, Alison Sprout, Rebecca Donner, Mira Jacob, Joanna Yas, Ellen Miller, Amanda Robb, and Elizabeth May.

For permission to quote his poetry and beautiful self, thanks to Peter Nickowitz. I am deeply grateful to the Sewanee Writers' Conference for bringing into my life so many of the people who abetted this book; to Arlie Hochschild for igniting my curiosity about female imagery; to Rosette C. Lamont for introducing me to portraits and self-portraits of artists in words; to Louis Menand for guiding me to my modernist heroes; and to Francine Cournos for encouragement beyond compare. For Why not? and other permissions, I thank Michael Cunningham.

This book exists because of the amazing Frances Coady, who read my intentions with perfect understanding. I cannot imagine a more astute and playful editor. Georges Borchardt invited me on this journey with the same words with which my father proposed to my mother; his belief in me makes me enormously proud and diligent. I am grateful to Anne Borchardt as well.

Without my husband, Ricardo Zurita, joy, fun, tenderness, all good things would swirl intangibly around me.